SOMETHING NAUGHTY

DELILAH DAWSON

St. Martin's Paperbacks

This is a work of fiction. All of the characters, organizations and events portrayed in this novel are either products of the author's imagination or are used fictitiously.

SOMETHING NAUGHTY

Cover photo © Hywel Jones/getty

ISBN: 0-312-93655-9
EAN: 978-0-312-93655-6

Printed in the United States of America

St. Martin's Paperbacks edition / January 2007

St. Martin's Paperbacks are published by St. Martin's Press, 175 Fifth Avenue, New York, NY 10010.

10 9 8 7 6 5 4 3 2 1

prologue

Edible bra and panties? But we sell business suits!" Damon Becker turned squarely to face his grandmother.

"And now, edible underwear, honey," Henrietta replied, frowning at him. "Women aren't exactly rushing in to buy our suits, so it's time to give them an incentive." She reached for the bottle of lotion to sniff it.

Damon couldn't believe it. "With who?"

His grandmother's weak smile only fed the dread in his gut. "With Naughty Devil. I'm sure you've heard of them. They are a small company just like us, but they carry very nice stuff. Intimate women's apparel and such."

"Are you saying we're going from three-piece business suits to . . ." He gestured at the merchandise spread on the table in disbelief. "This? We have a solid reputation in our business—"

"Which is all fine and dandy, but it's time for a change," she said firmly. "These items are sexy and tasteful." Her smile reappeared and she inspected the package of edible lacy underwear. "Perhaps literally."

He bit back a groan. Holy Christ.

"Opportunity presented itself, Damon. I couldn't let it pass us by." She wiggled her eyebrows at him. "I'm positive this is going to work out. What better way than to mix a little naughty with a whole lotta nice?"

"Please tell me you're kidding."

She continued, unconcerned. "This is evolution, kiddo. Change is good. What do you think of 'Whether you're in or out of a suit, in Becker Fine Tailoring, you'll always look stunning.' Kinda wordy, but you get the gist, right?"

He steepled his fingers and leaned in, trying to center his thoughts and follow hers. "We have four generations' worth of conservative reputation—"

"They were *my* ancestors before they were yours, Damon." A half-turn from where she sat was enough to remind him that despite being eighty-two years of age and in fragile health, she still called the shots. "I've made many decisions without your help, thank you very much."

Had her new medication for her heart condition pushed her past her normal levels of eccentricity?

She pointed an emerald feather tickler at him. "Just because my heart is sputtering along doesn't mean my mind is gone!"

Damon felt a moment of guilt. He'd deliberately stayed out of the family business, making his visits short so as not to be dragged into it. Being on tour duty in the army had made much of that possible. Now, he was home. To this.

"Nana, I wish you would've brought me in on the decision sooner."

"Don't be silly. You weren't even in the country. Anyway, it's a reputable, distinguished business and . . . what's done is done. We're now in the naughty business, or rather, they're in ours."

He covered her hand, feeling the frail bones that had held the reins to the business for so long. "It's not too late. Give me a couple of days to find a loophole."

"I can't, Damon. I won't. In fact, I'm looking forward to it."

He kept his mouth shut to hold back his disagreement. He felt inexplicably torn; the tailoring business had been the pain and pride of his family for as long as he could remember.

"Promise me you'll help make this a smooth transition," she insisted.

"I haven't seen all the products yet—"

"Oh, try not to be so starchy! What works for Naughty Devil should also work for us. Mixing our formal style with a little of the Naughty Devil titillation is just the right combination. Sexy and vibrant. I'm not so old that I've forgotten what that's about."

Her hand fluttered over her chest and he felt a moment of sheer panic. "Are you okay?"

"Relax." She frowned. "I was just sensing Jamus nearby."

Great. Now Grandpa's ghost was in the room?

Her features softened and she patted his cheek. "My father and his father's father, and his beyond that, built this business into what it is today. I want to leave my mark too, Damon. This is my legacy. You will help make it happen, won't you?"

If her speech hadn't convinced him, the faint moisture in her eyes left him no choice. It tore him up inside to see it. He couldn't remember ever seeing her near tears. She had never seemed so fragile and small.

He nodded.

"Promise?" she insisted.

"Have I ever contradicted you and won?" he hedged.

Her smile crept back and she stubbornly blinked the moisture away. "Excellent. I'll set up a meeting."

chapter 1

"This lotion is lightly lubricating, and the floral scent is not overpowering. Would you like to try it?"

Tanika Davis extended the bottle to Damon Becker's open hand and a droplet accidentally spilled over, landing in his palm.

"Oops! I'm sorry." She looked around for tissue but he was already crushing the dab of cream with his hands as if it were paper he could crumble.

"Sorry about that," she apologized.

He mumbled something she couldn't quite hear.

Tanika hurried to put the top back on, briefly wished her sister was in her shoes to handle the situation, rather than still at the hospital, happily nursing her brand-new baby. At the moment, twenty-seven hours of labor didn't sound so bad. It beat the heck out of doing a sales pitch to the Patron Saint of Propriety.

Her first impulse when she met him was to drag him into the nearest closet and uncork her sexual frustrations. Three seconds later she realized he had the personality of a butler. And it was definitely not the kind that made hot monkey love in supply closets.

"Need a tissue?" she asked politely when he continued to rub his palms together.

"No, thanks."

His head was clean-shaven, his features were roughly attractive, and his skin absolutely flawless. To top it off, he was wearing a black suit that looked perfect in the light. He had the intensity of a preacher and the brawniness of a linebacker. Truth be told, she was having trouble getting past his body.

Mmm, mmm, good!

But when he steepled his fingers like that, he looked painfully allergic to the slightest sin.

"If the lotion's not your type, don't worry. It's a subtle scent that washes off with soap. But if you like it, all it needs is a little body heat to linger." She smiled, hoping he'd show some levity.

To no surprise, she watched him across the narrow boardroom table as he glanced sternly down at the stack of papers before him. "There are products here that are anything but subtle, Ms. Davis."

Brother. Was he for real? "Actually, Naughty Devil offers a range of products, from the elegant and, yes, subtle, to the bold and sassy."

He pointed to the array of products before him. "We could start with the lingerie and exotic lotions, but the other kinky toys do not belong in a women's clothing store."

Kinky? Not unless his clients were all monks, and even then! Had no one ever used a little fun-bondage on this guy?

"We only carry a handful of 'toys,' and they are only available online. These velvet handcuffs are hardly kinky, Mr. Becker," she said with a careful smile. She glanced at his large hands, certain the velvet would be snug and tight around his wrists, but they would fit. Maybe behind his back instead of the headboard, but—

He gave her a look that seemed to read her thoughts.

"My clientele would consider them playful," she said, holding tight to her smile.

The slightest furrow of his brow was comment enough.

Deciding not to fall into the trap of explaining herself, Tanika took a large gulp of her cooling coffee, then charged on. "As a matter of fact, high-level executives make up a large percentage of our repeat customers, and not just for lotions and lingerie. It's why your VP asked me to work with you on an advertising strategy."

His frown deepened. "I've looked over your product selection and I don't see a simple way to blend them in the catalog. I propose we keep half the catalog for the Becker Apparel items and half for ND items. We can even print one catalog upside down from the other, give them a little juxtaposition. How does that sound?"

"Mutual placement is the key, Mr. Becker. A marketing strategy has already been discussed with your grandmother."

He leaned back, his shoulders holding his tension like boulders. He looked like he was about to say something but instead he briefly nodded his shaven, perfectly shaped head, looking resigned. "I see."

Tanika felt a twinge of pity for him. "I was expecting to meet with your grandmother, the CEO, today."

He leaned back. "She asked me to convey her apologies for not being able to attend. However, she wanted me to review the ads, if you have them."

"I do."

"Then by all means, please continue."

He didn't have to look like she was requesting a prostate exam, for crissake.

"Is there a problem?" he asked.

She widened her stiff smile. "Actually, there was. We couldn't book our original model, and because of time restrictions, we substituted. Perhaps another meeting with your grandmother would be—"

"Ms. Davis." He leaned forward again, all wide shoulders and intensity stretched taut. "I'm sure the model you chose will do nicely."

Hmm. "Of course."

His eyes narrowed ever so slightly at her tone of voice.

She tapped her pencil in her hand. "Well, then . . ."

* * *

*D*amon noticed Tanika's tone didn't change one bit, but she looked distinctly annoyed. Her attitude emanated from her in waves, sparking in her eyes.

Dazzling eyes. Sultry. Like dark amber in sunlight. Despite her business suit, luscious curves, and a perfectly conservative French knot, her eyes were the epitome of seductive temptation. Everything about her was so unmistakably feminine. There was nothing he could put his finger on precisely, just a natural comfortable sensuality about her body, an unconscious femininity that was almost blatantly sexual . . . and yet wasn't.

She quietly cleared her throat and he briefly refocused on the pen in his hand as he listened to her.

"We market our products with the Naughty Devil logo, so here are some ideas of how I would approach joint placement in ads. As you will see, our products are not as incompatible as you'd think."

Tanika placed a large portfolio case on the table. The sand-brown tailored jacket she wore was molded to the lush roundness of her breasts and a faint satin-on-satin sound reached his ears. The barest scent of an unknown fragrance wafted over to distract him. Lily? No, that was too soft. Definitely not roses. Orchids? Musk? No, greener. What was it?

"Here is a glimpse of *our* hosiery and one of *your* suits." She straightened a photo of a man in a Becker Fine Tailoring suit, hands fisted in his trouser pockets as if to hide an erection in his pants. He boldly stared at the camera with an almost thuglike challenge.

A woman hid behind him, eyes laughing as she peered over his shoulder wearing reading glasses, pencils sticking out of her coiffure. Halfway down, the angle of the shot showed off one of her legs, long, sensuous, and encased in thigh-high black nylons . . . all the way down to the burgundy high-heeled pumps. Sexy.

The laughing eyes halted him. Amber eyes. "You?"

"Well, as I mentioned, I thought I was going to meet with your grandmother. I no longer do modeling work—"

"You were a model?"

"Mostly for size twelve. Obviously not for anything less. But anyway, we had a booking conflict, so . . ." She sighed. "I was assured this would not be an issue."

He looked back at the photo, studying the very long, very sexy leg. "No. Not an issue." Right. Sure. Was getting a hard-on considered an issue?

"Should I continue?"

He nodded. "By all means."

She turned to the next photo and didn't bother with an explanation.

It didn't need one.

The body shot of a woman pushed back on the edge of a desk was graphic enough. Her plaid

Becker skirt was around her hips, the photo showing just enough of her bare inner thigh to titillate. A man in pin-striped Becker trousers stood between her legs, the belt dangling suggestively. At the point where the skirt gathered at her hips, a tiny tattoo of the Naughty Devil peeked out. Damon felt instantly transported into the picture, dry-mouthed and shocked by the rush of blood to his groin. He could practically feel the heat of her vagina against his cock.

The apt tagline "You can have it on his desk by the end of the day" was written in red cursive.

Sweet Mother of Moses!

"Here's a shot of the lingerie," she continued.

In it, Tanika lounged in an executive chair in nothing but a Becker trench coat. She was speaking into a microrecorder in her hand and studying a thick open binder in her lap, seemingly oblivious to how the coat fell open to reveal the curve of a lace-covered breast and torso. Her mouth was parted, just inches from where her red-tipped nails held the microrecorder, the gloss on her lips inviting unscrupulous thoughts. The caption read "Dictation method no. 5."

He forced himself not to shift in his seat.

He was tempted to bring the image closer and study that perfect mouth, but she turned to the next ad. It invited blow job fantasies. Damn . . .

And there she was again but this time in a gym shower. She stood with her back to him, naked but for a man's shirt—Becker, no doubt—and tight-knit fishnet stockings and garters. The cotton shirt looked deliciously translucent in the places where the shirt touched her skin, like wet icing. The damned tattoo appeared again on her thigh, just under the rippling crease of water. Was it real? The close-up shot captured the chill on her skin and made him want to run his hand over the photo and warm her, caress her . . .

"This one is for what you would refer to as kinky items."

The photo looked like it had been taken in an elevator. A man's broad back could be seen as he faced a corner, his long, signature Becker trench coat almost touching the ground. The only visible sign of Tanika was her hands at his neck, one clutching the coat near his collar in a desperate grip and the other cupping his head. A velvet handcuff dangled from her wrist. The coat bulged oddly at the waist, giving the impression that her legs were intimately wrapped around the man's waist. No doubt she was naked. Straining to take him in an illicit moment of fornicating passion.

The caption read "Want to hold a captive audience?"

For the elevator camera?

Damon's erection hardened further, pushing uncomfortably in his trousers. It didn't help that the identical trench coat was draped on the arm of the empty chair next to him. Same color too.

The drumming of his pulse was deafening. This wasn't an ad to sell sophisticated clothes.

She spoke again, her voice unfailingly polite but almost bored. "And this last one targets the lotions."

In it, she sat at a mirrored vanity wearing an over-sized man's shirt. White. The collar sagged enough to reveal a Becker Fine Tailoring tag in the back. The shirt was unbuttoned halfway down to reveal a hint of her full breasts.

Behind her was the out-of-focus view of a rumpled bed . . . with a man in it. She was licking her lips while one of her hands hovered over the vast selection of lotion bottles before her, her face beaming with rushed excitement. As if the choice she had to make had to be quick. Naughty. Tasty.

The caption was "Decisions! Decisions!"

"Well?" she asked politely.

No. Absolutely, positively not!

"It's definitely . . . different," he muttered. "Our approach has always been to present fashion with a little less scandal and instead place the focus on the professional aspects, Ms. Davis."

Her eyebrows shot up. "I don't see anything truly scandalous about these ads. There's lots of implied passion, but that doesn't translate to scandal."

He pointed to the desk, elevator, and shower ads. "Our last ad had our models reading the *New York Times* by a warm fireplace."

"I'm sure that can be arranged," she murmured, looking entirely too innocent. "I'll pass it along."

Yeah, I'll bet. Without a doubt his forefathers were doing triple flips in their graves. "The point of a good ad is to get more customers, not alienate them or blindside them," he pointed out.

"I concur." She mimicked him by tapping her pencil in her hand, and he got the distinct impression she was mocking him. "However, we're going for a younger, more energetic demographic, Mr. Becker. We need to market ourselves to stand out. Becker Fine Tailoring and Naughty Devil. The women's line of suits and the Naughty Devil products are a match made in heaven. The best way to blend the two is with the Naughty Devil logo. We can pull it off."

He wanted to shift his erection into a more comfortable position or simply unzip and save the big fella from the stranglehold it was in, but that was not going to happen, so he decided to cut to the chase.

"Resorting to selling sex is not what Becker Fine Tailoring is about, Ms. Davis."

She gave him a cool, predatory look. "Well, Naughty Devil is all about selling *the possibility of sex,* Mr. Becker. That has the most lasting impression. We want to make the client feel professional yet provocative and sensual. Confidence stems from that. People love the possibility of sex, the chemistry, the foreplay, even if they are stuck in a boardroom for four hours, wearing an uncomfortable, stuffy suit with a stellar reputation."

"Stuffy?" he asked calmly. "Are you saying

Becker Fine Tailoring makes stuffy suits?" The men who had served under him in the army would have recognized the warning in his voice, but she apparently didn't.

"Of course not." But her denial was mocked by her eyes. "I'm simply saying that sexual allure is a common marketing ploy that we intend to leverage to create a new image for the Becker Fine Tailoring line."

"There's nothing wrong with the old image. If anything, there is a certain nostalgic, romantic element there. We offer the finest quality, use top-of-the-line materials, and have—"

"Zero sex appeal."

He wanted to stand, lean over, and impress on her the integrity and sacrifice of four generations of custom tailoring that demanded to be defended. But sporting a raging hard-on probably wasn't going to help him with this argument. So he stayed seated and silently fumed.

"It's as simple as this, Ms. Davis. Becker suits give people an edge in a business encounter by making a distinct professional statement."

"And that's working extremely well for your men's line. But for your women's line, not so much." Tanika started to put her inventory of lotions, edible underwear, and sundry items into her briefcase. "Mr. Becker, we will see more sales if people purchase both of our products with the hope that their business—whether in the courtroom or the bedroom—involves some sensuality or even erotic pleasure. Don't you agree?"

And there, he decided, was the problem. "Business and pleasure don't mix."

Again the quick, disbelieving look. "Ideally, in theory, that may be true, but never in advertising. In any case, what's wrong with giving your customers another reason to buy your suits?"

He gave her the once-over. "Is that why *you* buy a suit?"

She froze in mid-motion, and he knew he'd surprised her.

"You're wearing one of our best suits," he noted. "Did you buy it to be sexy and alluring or to present a professional image at this meeting?"

Instead of showing embarrassment, a flash of sensual fire lit her eyes, mentally knocking him on his ass. Her gaze held, starting a phantom caress that swirled like satin through and around the thickness of his penis before settling in his testicles.

"Well, that goes toward my point," she said carefully. "Do you want to know what I'm wearing underneath all this? Are you curious to know which of the various Naughty Devil lotions or lingerie I decided on this morning? Does any of that matter to you or do you prefer to think of this as a dry-cleaned suit with fine tailoring?"

Images of what might be under her double-breasted jacket seared his mind. Her scent was still eluding him, but was no less haunting for it.

"I'd rather avoid a sexual harassment lawsuit than answer that," he replied.

She placed a few more items into her briefcase, sighing patiently, and he felt like a child who wasn't understanding basic math. "Our customers won't have to vocalize their thoughts, Mr. Becker. It's enough to make them wonder *whether* I could be wearing the Pink Dahlia lotion, or *whether* I chose to slip on item number fifty-nine twenty under this suit today. That's our selling point."

From earlier research of the ND products, he remembered the "fifty-nine hundred" selections were satin camisole-and-thong combos. His imagination went into overdrive.

"And wondering what a woman wears under her suits is not completely sexist," she continued breezily. "For that matter, women will wonder whether the men who wear your suits might also use one of our many unisex lotions, or if they have on our tuxedo boxer shorts or . . . whatever else. Statistics prove sexual speculation is part of human nature."

She closed her briefcase with a definite click and a business card fluttered to the floor. She bent to retrieve it and Damon tilted his head to admire the curve of her luscious butt . . . and the way the suit molded to it.

Booty-bountiful!

And to think there was a red thong under that suit, just waiting to show off the sexy round mounds of her sweet behind and—

She straightened, smiled at him, and tucked the card into her breast pocket, her eyes gleaming victoriously.

He wanted to smack himself on the forehead.

"Are we in agreement about the marketing strategy, then?" she asked sweetly.

He smiled in spite of his straining erection. "Not entirely. I still think that, human nature or not, we should consider toning it down, make ripples in the advertising rather than a splash."

She seemed amused again, which irked him even more. "Mr. Becker, this is more of a formality. Your grandmother bought into the ideas when I spoke with her on the phone and she hadn't seen the photos yet. I'm fairly confident she plans on moving forward with them as they are."

He checked a flare of impatience, both for Tanika and his grandmother. "If this was a done deal, I could've spent my time on other urgent matters, Ms. Davis."

She lowered her coffee mug and her smile suffered. "My job is to acquaint you with the less tangible aspects that make Naughty Devil so popular, its sensual, and yes, provocative, spirit. If we are to succeed in this marketing strategy, I hope you will evaluate and approve of *our* products as completely as we do *your* apparel—"

"I understand where you are coming from, but Becker Fine Tailoring does have a reputation to maintain," he stated firmly.

"Be that as it may, your current 'reputable' marketing plan is not showing a profit. Our partnership will serve to expand the women's line of Becker Fine Tailoring and introduce our products along with it. And as you can clearly see, my company also has a reputation to maintain. I can assure you that we are not suffering from loss of profit." Her curt reply seemed like a judge's gavel hammering into the following silence.

He held her gaze knowing she would continue with her sex-crazed agenda either with him or without him. Hell, she had a huge point there. But more importantly, he'd promised his grandmother he'd cooperate, right? At the very least, he wasn't supposed to jeopardize things.

"All right," he conceded after a long pause.

It was worse to see the pity back in her eyes. "Mr. Becker, I'm optimistic this will work. In fact, I'll tell you what I tell all my customers. 'Delve into the experience.' It's the Naughty Devil motto."

"Ah, yes. Catchy."

"Well, unless you get into our toys, in which case it changes to 'Naughty Devils Do.' "

Oh, sweet Jesus. Was there anything Naughty Devil didn't do? "I must not have received that catalog," he said.

"Not a problem. I'll get one to you. Our quarterly report should reflect the growing success. However, I strongly suggest you do more than just evaluate the chemical makeup of our lotion or measure the fiber count in our lingerie. Try out our products. See what you like or don't like. Rub on some lotion and see if it itches. Try our boxer shorts and report back any problems. After all, I've taken this approach with your products."

"And you found them stuffy?"

"I'd never say such a thing, Mr. Becker."

He was about to reply when a polite knock at the door had them turning to it. Mrs. Merriweather, his secretary, stood with keys and purse in hand. "I apologize for the interruption, but I wanted to let you know I'm on my way out."

"Thanks, Helen," he said. "I'll lock up."

"By the way, sir, I'll be off tomorrow, but I'll be at the holiday party in the evening."

"Great. I'll see you then."

After a chorus of goodbyes, Tanika tossed her Styrofoam cup into the trash and reached for her purse and briefcase. "It's late. I should get going, too."

He glanced at his watch, mentally groaning at the unfinished work sitting on his desk. Hell, it would still be there tomorrow. "If you'll wait just a minute, I'll leave with you."

When she turned away, Damon took advantage of the moment to slip on his coat, effectively hiding his arousal. Not since high school had he had such an uncontrolled hard-on.

On the way out, he paused to set the office alarm, then lock the door.

They entered the elevator together. The piped-in music was playing some punched-up jazz. He frowned. Just yesterday it had played tunes that belonged in malls and fitting rooms. Conservative music that inspired shopping and suited Becker Fine Tailoring to a T.

She pressed the button and waited as the doors silently slid shut.

Damon tried to ignore the fact that she stood in a corner and he was wearing his full-length coat. The vivid elevator ad refused to leave his mind. Now that he thought about it, he'd never had sex in an elevator before. Nor in his office. The possibilities suddenly bloomed in the tension, taunting him.

He absently rubbed his jaw and encountered the erotic scent she'd accidentally dropped into his palm.

The elevator began its descent.

Tanika knew it was an optical illusion, but Damon Becker seemed to take up too much space in the elevator. She resisted checking her French knot from her reflection in the wall of brass and instead kept both hands gripped on her briefcase handle.

It was too easy to imagine Damon pinning her against the corner while she wrapped her cuffed hands around his broad shoulders.

Man, oh man . . . his body was just made for stuff like that.

It was one thing to do a photo shoot with a gay model and quite another to imagine the real thing with a straight man who looked like Damon.

Maybe she'd forget the handcuffs and kiss him until she had his perfectly creased trousers unzipped and pushed down mid-thigh. Oh, she'd stroke him all right. She might even introduce him to some oral delights.

Too bad he wasn't her type. Her sex life had no room for uptight, prim, and humor-impaired men.

It wasn't as if she couldn't get a date. But who wanted that scene anymore? The last guy she'd dated had become clingy and needy, obsessed with "where's this relationship going" questions until she'd called it quits. He hadn't taken it well at all and the whole thing had turned into a huge mess.

Being a heartbreaker was a bitch.

As a result, it was wiser and far less complicated to just enjoy a rare one-nighter. No muss, no fuss. Just hit-and-run sex and bam, move on.

But now, the sexual hiatus had her hormones totally rebelling, the sexual urges taking on an edge of desperation.

Not that Mr. Propriety over here had picked up on it.

"What scent is this?" Damon asked, sniffing his open hand.

The instant thought that came to mind was of his fingers gripping his hardened erection, taking

his time sliding back and forth in languid mastur-
bation . . . God, he couldn't mean *that* scent! The
glint in his eye told her he'd read her mind. Again.
It took a split second more to remember that she'd
accidentally spilled a drop of lotion on him.

"Pink Dahlia," she replied huskily, before clearing her throat. "One of our bestsellers from the
flower series. We have nine."

"It's, um, interesting. You're wearing it," he said,
surprising her with his low rumble of certainty.

"Am I?" She absently straightened her jacket.
"This is exactly what our marketing strategy is about,
Mr. Becker. Raising the possibility."

He moved closer to her, slightly crowding her. He
was smart enough to leave room for her to move
away if she chose.

"What are you doing?" she demanded.

"Delving into the experience, as you suggested."
When she didn't move away, he shifted closer still.

Taken by surprise, she was rooted to the spot
as he lowered his head and inhaled at the base of
her neck, his nose barely nudging her small hoop
earring.

Her eyes drifted shut and an involuntary shiver of
delight melted down her spine.

"Yes," he said gruffly, "you are wearing it."

For a breath of eternity, his eyes locked on hers
and she felt like she'd fallen slowly into water,
steadily sinking. Her own quiet panting echoed in

the small space. She caught a whiff of his subtle cologne as it wrapped around her. Sophistication, wrapped up in manliness and eight hours' worth of starched cotton and body heat.

Very erotic. And unexpected. She'd have to think of how to bottle that.

She had the sudden urge to tug him by his tie and French-kiss the hell out of his firm mouth. Too bad he was Mr. Uptight.

"What's too bad?" he murmured.

His words began to penetrate the hazy fog as the elevator came to a stop and the doors retracted. God, had she really started to say that aloud? "Um, I said, not bad. Your sense of smell, that is."

He was still watching her too closely, too intimately. Definitely testing her.

Not one to back down, she leaned closer still and whispered, "Pink Dahlia is just the start. We have lots of other lotions. Some flower. Some musk. Others naughty and some kinky. You will want to delve into those, too."

His eyes darkened with the unmistakable sign of desire. "Ms. Davis—"

"Yes?"

She could practically see the words tottering on the tip of his tongue. But he held them back, hovering for a dangerous second before taking a step back. Something about the way he moved made her think of a panther, pretending to be held at bay by a little stick. It was just a matter of time before he'd prowl again.

"One more thing," he rumbled.

"Yes?" she repeated, her voice entirely too breathy.

"The item you mentioned earlier. Number fifty-nine twenty? It is a crimson-red camisole-and-thong combo with a black lace trim."

He barely glanced down at her suit, but she felt as if she were standing before him in only the items he'd mentioned. The fact that he was dead right send heat rushing over her that had nothing to do with embarrassment. "Very good."

His reply came at her like a brief intimate kiss. "Thank you."

The elevator doors automatically began to slide back together, but he stopped them with a press of a button, becoming the reserved businessman again. "After you."

Tanika walked out, her legs not quite steady. It was silly, really, to feel so annoyed with herself for wishing he'd had less control. For wishing he'd done something out of character, like kiss her or fuck her brains out in the isolated elevator . . . whatever. Maybe he wasn't into quickies.

He followed, half a step behind.

At the main entrance to the building, she nodded to the guard who held the door open for them.

She dug in her purse for her keys, grateful that she'd been allowed to park in the "Reserved" slot nearby.

"Good night, Mr. Becker." She used the remote

control in her key chain to unlock her yellow sports car.

"Good night."

He too used his remote control. It figured his car was the pristine black SUV parked next to hers.

She pasted on a smile and settled into her car, still juggling the fact that he'd turned her on more than she'd expected. Oh, yes, he was definitely good at starting a slow, smoldering burn.

With a twist of her wrist, the engine of her car roared to life, its ferocity joining the wildness he'd sparked in her. Two blocks later, she hit the freeway and, despite the cold December air, let the convertible top down while she gunned the engine into the fast lane.

chapter 2

The hotel ballroom was spectacular, and the weekend company Christmas party was already in full swing.

Damon was glad to see that employees from both companies were laughing and raising the level of conversation to the point that the slick-haired crooner with the band could barely be heard. Everyone was dressed to the nines and the dim light cast a romantic mood that was furthered by the full-window view of the winter garden.

Even now, Damon realized, he couldn't quite cut loose with his co-workers. His lips hurt from smiling and offering various greetings. He could see confusion in the eyes of the loyal workers who had contributed to Becker Fine Tailoring's distinction through the years.

He finished his drink, his gut instinct warning him he only had a few months to either earn their respect with this new venture, or disappoint them permanently. They obviously adored his grandmother, and were probably wondering if he was getting ready to take over.

Forcing the thought away, he focused on tracking the sleek, curvy woman who had him rethinking trench coats and elevators.

Tanika Davis wore a frosty pink evening gown that gleamed from her choker all the way to her ankles. The long slit on the side allowed for glimpses of her incredible legs, and the snug waistline completed the stunning look.

Instead of a French knot, her hair was pinned up in one of those fussy numbers that made a man want to take it down entirely and spread it on his pillow. Which was probably why he found himself constantly thinking about elevators, shower stalls, and desktops.

He'd been walking around in a state of semi-arousal ever since their meeting.

That dollop of lotion had not washed away as she'd promised. Or rather, he hadn't been able to get the scent out of his mind while masturbating in the shower. It had been a dangerous weakness to fantasize about her with her skirt around her hips on his desk, that sultry mouth of hers on his, maybe even whispering something naughty . . .

Damon watched her on the dance floor where the crowd allowed for little more than wiggling room. Out of nowhere, the memory of silk on silk replayed in his mind. His penis twitched. What lotion was she wearing today?

Disgusted with himself, he reached into his breast pocket for a cigar, then took a shortcut to a private alcove leading to the side garden. Cigars were a rare treat, but one he'd been saving for the New Year's celebration, still a week away.

He stepped through the double doors into the cool night breeze, glad to find himself alone. With a flick of his thumb a flame danced on the lighter and he held it to the tip of the cigar.

A few strong puffs thickened the smoke and sent it curling into the air. He watched the red glow, feeling an odd tug in his heart from knowing the occasion wasn't a celebration. He was done with the army, as much as anyone could be done with weapons and war. But this work, the one thing he knew he could count on to be sane and stable, seemed somehow tainted now, irrevocably altered. He could hardly get his thoughts around it.

Damon sighed, practically feeling four generations of ghosts standing beside him, lingering in the Cuban smoke, contemplating the changes in the upcoming year. Even the empty patio furniture reflected his sentiments.

Hell, maybe he shouldn't have had the third shot of bourbon. Despite the party music thumping through the windows, he felt a million miles away, and for several minutes, he cloaked himself in shadows and solitude.

The music momentarily grew louder when the door opened behind him. He turned to see Tanika

Davis stepping out into the cold, closing the door at her back.

"Well, there you are! You're a tough one to find. Brr, it figures you'd be out here."

What the hell did that mean? He clamped the cigar between his teeth and had his jacket off and around her shoulders before she'd taken another step.

She slipped her arms into the sleeves and hugged it close. "Oh, that's wonderful. Thank you. Actually, I only intended to pass on a message from your grandmother. She says she's tired and heading home early. She wanted me to stress that she was feeling perfectly fine."

He'd seen his grandmother dancing earlier as if her doctor hadn't warned her about overexertion. She'd grinned and waved at him with all that bittersweet trust in her eyes.

He'd have to check on her.

"Thanks." He waited for Tanika to leave, and felt a little restless when she didn't.

"Cuban?" she asked.

He exhaled smoke and nodded.

"I haven't had a cigar in ages. Do you mind?"

"Mind what?" he mumbled around his cigar.

She carefully reached for it, her warm fingertips brushing his lips in the process.

He watched in mute fascination as she brought it to her mouth and sucked. Her cheeks hollowed as she inhaled, her eyelids drifted half-shut, and he was suddenly and fiercely envious of the contact.

She handed the cigar back and he took it, tasting traces of her lipstick as he took a puff. The edginess he was fighting sank like claws into his gut, making him crave something more than just sensuous smoke and a cold dark night.

She snuggled further into his jacket, which was entirely too big for her. She looked good in it, though, a little helpless, a little sexy.

"You should go back inside where it's warm," he warned.

Her eyes studied his face and held there. He didn't bother hiding his hunger.

"Something bothering you?" she asked.

"Tell me, Ms. Davis, are you here to educate me on another scent that needs delving into?" He watched her through a puff of smoke. "Would you like me to guess what you are wearing under that dress, or maybe what lotion you used this evening?"

Her chin tipped up just slightly. Enough to catch the light in her dark amber eyes and reveal the rapid pulse at her throat.

"Getting into the spirit of Naughty Devil, huh?" she murmured.

If she only knew . . .

"I could quiz you on the Puro Moreno," she teased.

"Latin Lotion number five. With hints of coffee, chocolate, and traces of tobacco. It's another favorite among ND's clientele."

"Men especially." She smiled. "So much progress in such a short time. I'm impressed."

He extinguished the cigar on the small ashtray on the patio table. "Go in. You're starting to shiver."

He'd had coffee and chocolate mousse for dessert. And so had she. He was sure of it. And now the cigar. All the makings of a Puro Moreno. He wanted to delve into her mouth and taste her, and not for research purposes, either.

"Go in," he repeated.

"In a minute."

Her gaze locked on his and he felt like she held a fuse to him, sparking something somewhere that burned steadily with every second. Burned much too hot.

She stepped closer. "Go ahead," she whispered, running a finger down the side of her neck. "Guess which lotion I'm wearing."

Mentally muttering a curse, he slid his hands under the jacket to her waist and tugged her closer, then lowered his head and inhaled where she'd indicated.

Tanika withstood the assault of Damon's nose barely brushing against her skin as he searched out her scent. She endured the slow, controlled inhale and infinitely warmer exhale that had her shivering and gasping quietly.

She hadn't expected the lick on her pulse that turned into a molten heat in her veins. She couldn't contain her moan on the second lick, and she damn near melted when it turned into a kiss that seemed to tongue her very soul.

She slid her hand up his muscular arms and turned her head, needing only one thing. Damon's mouth slanted over hers almost savagely, taking her breath away with a hunger that nearly dominated hers.

She matched him in the tangled need, lost in the flavors of chocolate, coffee, and smoke they'd both sampled. His body felt rock hard against hers and she moaned, suddenly aware that her back was pushed against the brick patio wall.

She arched against the blatant bulk of his erection, the wall of his chest crushing her breasts, and she wanted to be closer still. Each kiss dove into the next until she was breathlessly dizzy, her mind spinning and her body aching.

Sheer necessity had her breaking for air. "Good God! Becker . . ."

He tilted his head back to the pulse at her throat, then after leaving a mind-tingling bite there, seemed to suddenly catch himself, reining in with impressive control.

"Shoulda gone inside," he said roughly.

Gathering her scattered thoughts took more effort than she'd imagined. "Yeah. Shoulda."

His eyes blazed with tightly held passion. They swept over her face, pausing at her lips. "I don't know."

She contemplated sucking his lips again. "Hmm?"

His voice was husky and as rough as a growl. "What you're wearing. I don't know it. Don't recognize the scent."

"Oh." Even though she'd spent ten minutes picking through the lotions for the night, her mind was too frazzled to bring up the name of even one. She watched his lips in stupefied fascination. God, he could kiss!

"I could very easily delve deep into you, Ms. Davis," he said gruffly. "More than delve, really."

Ohhhhh, yes, please . . .

"Tanika," she managed. Her nipples were pushing into his chest, his erection was all but jabbing her for entry, and he'd tongued her breathless and nearly senseless. A little informality seemed appropriate.

"Tanika," he repeated, warming each vowel on his tongue.

The dim outdoor light cast an off-kilter halo over his head, but caught the movement of a muscle twitching in his jaw. "I could blame it on the wine or the moonlight, but the damage is still the same. I never meant it to get so out of line."

Damage? Out of line? "I'm a big girl, Mr. Becker. I can handle a kiss."

He looked at her with a hunger that made her breath hitch. "I agree. You handled it expertly."

The soft yearning in her gut began melting deep inside.

"But . . ." He eased away with obvious regret, his imprint still scalding her body. "It's detrimental to a smooth working relationship, not to mention bad business practice."

Detrimental? Geez, the geek exec was back with his fifty-dollar words and lengthy explanations. What happened to the stranger who used words like "shoulda"?

"Detrimental, huh?"

"We are co-workers, Ms. Davis." Again the halo of light gleamed over his scalp as if perched precariously. "There's obviously a strong attraction between us, which, if you think about it, can be explained given the new business we now find ourselves in."

Goddammit! Was that what he thought of her? "I don't go around randomly kissing my business associates, Mr. Becker. I found you attractive and I kissed you. End of story. Truth be told, I was grappling with some pent-up energy, and under the circumstances, you happened to fit the bill."

His eyes became dark and as hard as flint. "Glad I could be of service," he gritted out. "Or do you still need me to complete the job?"

"Oh, please!" she snapped. "I'm a modern woman, Mr. Becker. I can admit to having sexual urges and acting on them. You, on the other hand, are obviously much more traditional—"

"Traditional?" His breathing evened out and his face became inscrutable.

"Yes." How had it come to this? "Apple pie, movies, wine and dine. That kind of thing."

He raised his eyebrow. "As opposed to . . . ?"

"Wild, spontaneous sex. Quickies. The modern approach."

"Like one-night stands?"

She wanted to sigh. "It's simply a difference in philosophy. I don't expect you to understand."

"Oh, I understand." He gave her lips another brief heated glance before continuing. "You're talking about no attachment. No real relationship. One-nighters are a perfect way to work someone out of your system and wake up the next day feeling like you'd played three good hours of serious racquetball."

Well . . . okay. For several seconds she toyed with the thought of working out that hard on his body. "Let me know when you get to the negative aspects."

His lips twitched with the ghost of a smile. "I don't do one-night stands." This time he put more distance between them, his gaze still pinning her to the wall. "Two-nighters or three-nighters maybe, but one is never enough."

Hot damn! Had he said what she thought he'd said? For a moment, she struggled not to gawk.

When her heart stopped jumping into her throat, she mumbled, "Okay."

His eyes narrowed. "I won't let sex get in the way of business," he stressed.

Well, tonight sex was the only urgent business she planned on dealing with. "Okay."

His intensity was almost overwhelming. "Does this mean we have an understanding?"

Excitement bubbled, threatening to overcome the control that had never failed her in the past.

"I understand we're about to have an affair," she said. "And just to avoid complications, when either one of us says it's over, *it's over.*"

He took his time mulling that in silence before saying, "All right."

For several seconds, there was only the thumping music and their ragged breaths to seal their deal.

Tanika almost screamed when a window was tapped nearby. They turned to see Ms. Merriweather with a shocked expression on her face. The secretary pasted on a smile and tapped her wristwatch at Damon. She then wiggled her fingers in goodbye, moving away from the window and disappearing as the curtain fell back in place.

"Damn." Tanika heard Damon's heartfelt mumble. "I asked her to let me know when the Richmonds were leaving," he said as he straightened. His erection was still noticeable.

Tanika slid out of his jacket, instantly shivering. "Ah."

"It's business." He opened the door and they stepped inside the warmth. He shrugged on the jacket, pausing to study her.

Standing half in the shadows, he seemed to

morph back into the cool exec before her very eyes, making her wonder if she'd imagined the passionate stranger who had propositioned her.

"Well, Ms. Davis, allow me to deal with Mr. Richmond and then we can continue our conversation," he said softly.

"I'd like that." What she really wanted to do was to squeeze her thighs together and ease the throb of arousal. Her breasts felt subtly swollen, enough that the slight friction from her dress chafed against her nipples.

She let Damon lead her back to the large ballroom, his warm hand tingling against her lower back. Once there, he lifted a champagne flute off the tray of a passing waiter, handed it to her, then with a polite nod melted into the crowd.

The sparkling bubbles did nothing to relieve the pent-up hunger. She could still feel his hard shoulder muscles, could feel the length of him pressing her against the wall.

Racquetball? Ha! More like wet rugby with a touch of wrestling.

It would be interesting to see which personality she would seduce. The gentleman or the stranger? The anticipation was already driving her crazy!

It was almost two in the morning before Damon left the hotel ballroom where lingering employees were heading home and the cleanup crew was getting started. Thoughts of his grandmother still lingered in the back of his mind, but she'd assured him, when he'd called, that she was just fine. That pretty much translated into "Don't you have better things to do?"

He sighed and rubbed his chin, already thinking about the upcoming night with Tanika.

. As much as he would've wanted to take her to his own home and into his bedroom, chances were she'd shy away from it. Probably think it was too personal, too emotional. As if sex tonight would be none of those things.

Impossible.

Reluctantly, he reserved one of the hotel's best suites, unable to suppress the feeling that she deserved better. He'd been halfway to the ballroom when he turned back to the lobby, picked up the courtesy phone, and called room service to have some appetizers and white wine brought up to the room.

At this rate, she was probably going to think he was a real pro at this.

He caught up with her in the hallway and, without a word, handed her the room key card. She tapped it once in her hand and smiled in that mysterious way that gave no clue to her thoughts.

He wanted to kiss her again, but didn't trust himself to stop there. Hell, he hadn't even trusted himself to dance with her.

"I'll be up in about five minutes," she said, then placed the key card into her tiny purse.

He nodded, reminding himself for the hundredth time that he was breaking a cardinal rule in business.

Mrs. Merriweather called him from the doorway and he looked over, wondering if she'd been shadowing him all night.

"I'll meet you upstairs," Tanika said, then moved on, heading for the elevators.

Damon walked over to where his secretary held a pen and paper for his signature. "Here's the last bill for signing," she explained.

He was writing when her husband strolled up. "Hey, Damon. Great night. Looks like everyone turned out."

"Both companies mingled well." He handed Mrs. Merriweather the pen and paper. "Did you guys have a good time?"

"Yes," her husband said with a genuine grin.

"The night's not over for some people," his secretary said through pursed lips.

Damon paused, surprised that the woman who had been nothing but motherly to him now sounded reproachful. "Be careful, Damon."

He knew what she was warning him about. Be careful not to destroy a relationship your grandmother has worked hard to build with Naughty Devil. Be careful not to destroy whatever respect the employees have for you if they find out you're sleeping with our latest business associate. Be careful that you're not thinking with your brain.

"Helen, don't meddle," her husband warned, placing an arm over her shoulder and smiling apologetically.

Mrs. Merriweather brushed her bangs aside, then fluttered her fingers. "Of course. Never mind me." But her eyes still flashed the warnings even as she smiled and said, "Good night."

After quick goodbyes the couple left, and Damon's doubts redoubled. He shoved his hands into his pockets, fingered the key card, and headed for the elevators.

He'd be careful.

The doors slid shut, closing out the world and isolating his turbulent thoughts. Tanika had been right about one thing. He was a traditional man. Mostly old-fashioned. His parents had been married for years until that fateful airplane accident. His grandmother too had been married for ages to Grandpa until that fatal heart attack.

Setting up a fling went very much against the grain. But then, the traditional family business had taken a turn, so why not him?

Where was the harm in a healthy night of passion? Yes, it had been a long time since he'd last had sex. Yes, this attraction was off the chain, but they were both intelligent, sexual adults.

Dammit, he wanted her. And that had nothing to do with any logic at all.

He pulled out the key card and tried to dig up another valid reason not to use it, but he could still taste her in his mouth. He could still smell her unique scent of a lotion he was no doubt supposed to identify. He wanted to taste her all over, to hear her beg for more, for him.

One night was a start. He'd already warned her he wouldn't be satisfied overnight. How he handled the rest would be tricky.

When the elevator doors opened, he stepped out and moved down the hall. He slid the card into the lock and heard the click of it disengaging.

Clamping down on his primal urges, he stepped into the room.

chapter 3

Tanika placed her purse and card key down on the glass coffee table and looked around the grand room, her eyes nervously skimming over the large bed with the turned-down sheets.

She rubbed the sudden ache in her gut. Lust, pure and simple. Why else was she here? To get the itch over with and get her groove on, that was all. Why turn down an opportunity to score some grade A sex?

The snick at the door had her turning to face it. Damon Becker, still looking impeccable in his tuxedo, stepped in. He hadn't even removed his bow tie, she noticed.

He closed the distance and placed his key card next to her purse. "Care for some wine?"

"Yes, please." She surprised herself by feeling tongue-tied and slightly out of her element.

She watched him check under the silver-domed dish that held appetizers, then reach into the ice bucket and pull out the wine. She'd rather see him serve the wine when he was naked, so she could stare at his ass, or even give it a feel. As it was, his erection was pressing on the front of his pants like a gift to be unwrapped. The very thought of tasting his erection while she covered it with champagne had her licking her lips.

Mmm-mmm . . .

The tension billowed, tempered only by the sound of the cork popping and the gurgle of white wine being poured.

He handed her the wine glass and poured himself one, too. Facing each other, they took a sip. His gaze was too heated for her to keep looking into his eyes, so she took a final sip of the cool tart liquid and placed her glass aside. If he was good, she'd play out her fantasy later . . .

He'd lowered his own wine glass enough that she reached for the black bow tie and tugged at it until it slipped around his collar to the floor.

"Much better," she murmured, still avoiding his gaze. She continued, sliding her hand under his jacket and pushing it over the roll of his left shoulder. His body heat enfolded her fingers as she skimmed the shirt.

Damon set his wine glass down and Tanika pushed the jacket completely off. It fell to the floor like a curtain.

His heart thundered beneath her palm and she finally looked up at him.

"Are you in a rush?" he asked.

"I don't see a point in lingering." If she had the strength, she would've ripped the shirt right off his firm body. Man, he was built like a friggin' statue. *Control yourself, girl. Don't scare him off with your wildness!*

"Want me to take it off?" he asked.

"No, I'll do it."

He swooped down and kissed her, softly, gently, with the quietest growl.

She clutched his shirt and tugged him closer, demanding more from the tender assault, then melting when he gave it to her. Each kiss became hungrier, more insistent, steadily tearing into her control with predatory skill. She lost herself in kisses, licks, and moans, until she was dizzy, clinging to the hard planes of his body for relief.

"Delicious," he said, his voice a dark and deep rumble. Without giving her a chance to respond, he kissed her again. Devoured her mouth until her lips felt puffy, bruised, and ready for more.

Tanika grappled with the buttons of his shirt, her uncoordinated fingers yanking at the expensive material. His hands eased from her face and skimmed the bare back of her dress, making the tingling aches in her breasts even stronger.

"Slow down, babe," he whispered against her lips.

What the fuck was up with his goddamned shirt? She made an involuntary sound of frustration and tried again. So help her, if it didn't give, she was going to screw him with his clothes on.

His rough chuckle broke the kiss and she looked up at him feeling nothing short of desperate. In spite of the passion blazing in his eyes, he looked oddly amused.

"I'll take the shirt off if you take that dress off," he rumbled huskily. "I can't find the goddamned zipper."

"Oh." Wow, he cussed. She felt much better. "Zipper's hidden." She reached for the right side of her dress, found it, and slid it down.

"Better yet," he said, "take it off nice and slow."

"Faster is better."

"No. Slow." The husky certainty in his voice left no room for argument.

God, any hot-blooded man would've had her on her back by now, and he wanted to take it slow? There was no spontaneity in slow!

She rubbed against him. "Fast."

He eased her back with a knowing grin. "Slow. Undress," he commanded, holding her gaze. "Come on, you can handle a slow pace, can't you?"

No, goddammit. No! "Of course."

His smile widened at the lie, and the flutter in her belly had her grappling for control.

She took a couple of steps back and started the show, undoing the tiny hook to the choker collar of the gown, then cupping the material over her breasts and easing it down, down . . . sashaying her hips slightly to get the dress further, the movement riding the satin of the thong against her wet clit. Biting her bottom lip to contain the pleasure, she released the dress to fall to the floor.

She knew the strapless bra didn't hide much and the thong even less. However, it was a personal favorite, pink and black. She'd been scantly dressed as a model before, but nothing and no one had made her feel as sexy as standing before him this way.

"Wow . . ." His shirt billowed with each breath he took and his erection had grown even larger against his pants. "Gorgeous . . . Turn around," came the gruff request. "No, no. Don't rush . . . Do it again, but do it slowly."

God, he was killing her! She turned again, pulling out the pins in her hair while making sure her high heels didn't damage the dress at her feet. She dropped the pins on the floor, letting her hair tumble to her shoulders, and waited.

He blasphemed quietly, in a hot dark voice that made a delicious shiver quiver up her spine.

"Your turn," she managed.

He looked up from the tiny devil tattooed on her thigh and tugged his shirt from his pants. In a slow deliberate pace, he undid each button, revealing tighter abs than she'd expected to see on a geeky exec. In a move worthy of a photo shoot, he stripped off the shirt and tossed it aside, revealing the arms and chest of a long-term athlete.

Tanika licked her lips. "Very nice."

"Ditto."

His erection jutted against his pants, twitching once as if to introduce itself.

She raised an eyebrow. "What are you waiting for? Take the rest off, Becker."

He grinned, wide and wicked. "You first. Start with the bra."

Tanika reached behind and undid the clasp. The pressure against her skin eased as the bra sagged. She let it fall, suddenly self-conscious about the weight of her full breasts and the imprint the bra had left on her skin. Her quarter-sized areolas were tightly aroused as the air hit them and the blood rushed to the very tips of her nipples.

Tipping her chin up, she crossed her arms under her breasts, trying to ward off the sudden coldness. "Your turn."

The belt buckle made a soft metallic sound, then slithered when it was pulled from the belt loops. The zipper teeth ate at the silence, then with a flex of his pecs and abs, he shucked his trousers, standing in gray pin-striped boxers and shoes.

Well, well. A glimpse of the geek, after all. Sexy! She licked her lips, her vagina clenching wetly.

He kicked off his shoes and took off his socks, then went to her. His legs were lean, sinewy, and tight, and even in her heels her head barely reached above his collarbone.

"Keep the high-heeled shoes on," he said, before pulling her into his chest and kissing her halfway out of her mind.

The heat of his skin on hers was explosive, the generous bulk of his erection even more. He cupped her bare buttocks almost roughly and pulled her hard against him. The scrap of her thong felt nonexistent against his cotton boxer shorts. His erection was already angled to penetrate, so she squirmed closer, needing it to the point that she wrapped a leg around him, wanting to climb him and take him deep into her.

Damon grunted something in her ear she didn't understand and a hard, breathless kiss later, she was tumbling onto the bed. He reached to the small of her back, and with an impatient tug, her thong fell apart.

His apology was muffled against her mouth. Her hands immediately went to tug off his underwear.

She didn't look. Didn't have to. She could smell the clean mustiness of him, his penis solid and thick against her belly. She wanted to ride him hard and fast, but he was too solid to be pushed onto the bed to do just that.

"Damon!"

"So impatient . . ." He shifted then rolled her onto the bed until they lay in the middle of it. Finally, *finally* their bodies aligned, his weight pinning her down, the tip of his cock nudging the folds of her vagina like a tongue.

"Please . . ." She shifted, digging her heels into the bed to take him.

"We have all night, babe."

Man, she couldn't believe she'd actually whimpered. "Fuck slow," she finally burst out.

"My point exactly." His fingers reached between her legs, over the swell of her mons, to delve past the soft, trimmed curls and into her sensitive sex. She jolted at the sensation of the contact, stilling as she was filled by first one, then two fingers. "We are going to fuck . . . slow."

Oh, God . . . oh, God!

He stroked her so beautifully, she felt incoherent when his thumb stroked her clit while his fingers dove into her vagina. The world narrowed to only that magical contact, the textured roughness of his fingertips swirled into her lubricated passage again and again, going in just deep and hard enough to get her to the edge, then backing off when he sensed her about to come.

Please! Oh, fuck, oh . . . "Damon!"

She almost cried out when he withdrew. Reacting blindly, she reached for his cock and stroked it once, leading it to her parted thighs, but he pulled her hands away with a groan and held them over her head.

"Stop rushing."

"I—I . . . have mercy . . . I need you . . ." Her voice was thin with desperation.

He shuddered slightly above her, as if her words had burned him. "Darlin' . . ." he murmured. In the blink of an eye, he had a condom packet in his hand and was using his teeth to tear it open. He rolled it on single-handed.

He kissed her hard, drinking in her moan as he took her, sliding inch by ribbed inch into her wet sheath until they were locked and docked together.

He turned his head and kissed her neck, his words low and husky and incomprehensible.

"Oh . . . Oh!" She sank her teeth into his shoulder, the voiceless lash of stark, mind-bending pleasure quivering and quaking in her gut as she clutched around him, feeling the tiny tremors of pre-orgasm.

"Tani . . . ka . . . God . . ." He surged into her . . . lips to mouths . . . cock into sheath . . . like tongued kisses . . . His hard cock impaled her, his thighs straining and nudging hers wider, then he shifted his cock impossibly deeper, every ribbed thrust wringing another growing spasm of pleasure from her.

Trapped in the emotions, she clung on, bracing. He rolled his hips, surging in and out at a vagina-tingling pace. Her pink-heeled shoes gleamed in the light as their bodies slapped together like waves crashing in a storm.

With her eyes shut, she could practically see his cock filling her like a piston, slick with her cream and getting rougher as his own control slipped. Her inner thighs trembled weakly, anticipating the roll of his hips as he ground his pelvis against her sensitive and aching clit.

Pleasure spiraled brightly behind her eyes, so close, so fucking close . . . "Ohhhh!"

With a hard gush of breath, she choked on a

scream and came mindlessly undone, shattering deep inside like slick quicksilver, her body gripping around him as the sweet wet orgasm tore through her with the force of a hurricane.

She couldn't help arching and tensed, her thighs clamping down, holding him fast against that magical orgasmic spot inside her, pumping out every delicious gut-clenching release until she was too weak to do anything at all.

Her legs slid back on the mattress, and in the aftermath, she became aware that Damon was still breathing hard, his shoulder muscles knotted and tense as he held perfectly still.

She turned her head and found him watching her with fire and amazement in his eyes. It dawned on her that he was clenching his teeth and sweating, his erection still rock hard. He released her captured hands and braced his forearms beside her ribs.

"Damon?"

Watching her intently, he thrust hard twice more, his cock seeming to swell just as he filled her with his hot ejaculation. With a rough grunt, he collapsed on her, his body still rocking and straining, salty sweat and tight muscles easing gradually, until he lay perfectly still on top of her.

He didn't smother her exactly. The feeling was too sensual and comfortable for that; his weight felt good. She ran her hands down his spine, trailing over the perspiration gathered there.

Lured by his calm breathing, she kissed his

shoulder and hummed her appreciation. Her heart hadn't quite stopped knocking hard, but then, neither had his.

Damon kissed her lips softly, then rolled over so that she now was lying on him. He smiled weakly at her and lazily cupped her left butt cheek with one hand. She smiled back, then settled against his chest and dozed off.

She snored. Damon grinned as he listened to the dainty yet unmistakable sound. He wouldn't have pegged her for a snorer, but then, he hadn't expected her to reach an orgasm in only sixty seconds, either. And what an incredible orgasm it had been to witness.

He'd never seen anything so . . . beautiful. The rush of it had swamped her features, tensing in her cheeks, her breath breaking between her parted lips, her sultry eyes dark with the peak of passion. Then the unmistakable clench of her body around him, wet and hot and succulent. Tight as a masturbating fist, as potent as a lover's mouth.

Her surrender had looked almost painful, but her moan had been filled with such exquisite pleasure. He was getting hard again just thinking about it . . .

He'd almost forgotten the condom.

He stared at the ceiling in disbelief, then resigned himself to wait to ask Tanika what she was using. He was almost sure she'd already thought of it, but almost forgetting contraception wasn't a mistake he intended to make again. But then, he'd never been that out of control before, either.

He tugged the blanket to cover them, but it snagged on the heel of her right shoe. He leaned up at an angle to check and felt a hit of satisfaction when he caught their reflection on the dresser mirror.

Her body, lean, curvy, and lighter brown, slumped over his darker body, accented by the silvery-pink high heels at her feet. She was a sensuous armful. Her hair fell all over his chest, her face stunning in sleep.

He leaned back down, branding the image into his mind. After a few minutes, he carefully used his feet to remove her shoes, then he turned her over, covered her with the blanket, and left the bed.

He needed to think.

Oddly revitalized, he took a quick shower and donned one of the courtesy robes available.

He stood by the side of the bed for a while, watching her sleep, and was tempted to wake her up with kisses. He was hooked and knew it. Had sex ever been *that* good before?

He rubbed his head, realizing that if he was going to be strategic about this relationship, he had to play it cool, show some restraint.

Intrigued to know more about her, he dialed the front desk. Fifteen minutes and an extravagant tip later, he'd handed his car keys to an attendant to retrieve the Naughty Devil sampler from the trunk of his car.

The teenager all but craned his neck to peer into the room when he dropped it off, but Damon blocked the view with his body, thanked him and firmly closed the door.

He settled the large metallic case on the coffee table, then selected some pear slices from the appetizer platter and refilled his wine glass.

Tanika embodied the Naughty Devil essence. So what secrets did she keep in the bottles?

Damon unlocked the case and slid open all the compartments, going directly to the tiny lotions. Each sample was neatly aligned, so he selected one, raising it to his nose for several seconds.

She'd seduced him with her body, her mind, and her scent.

The fragrances he'd detected on Tanika's body still haunted him as intimately as her orgasm. He reached for the next bottle, bound and determined to find out which of the lotions she'd dressed herself with.

chapter 4

Black Orchid."

The masculine whisper flittered into Tanika's dream and she smiled at the sensual tone, turning toward the sound. "Mmm?"

She peered through her lashes at Damon in time to see him flick the tip of her right nipple with his tongue, watching her. Her breast immediately responded to the contact, constricting tightly.

"And you have Black Pearl on your navel . . . and right here." His hand moved down her body, his fingertips resting right over her mons. His mouth still remained on her breast.

"Love the naughty little devil tattoo, by the way . . ."

Tanika was wide awake now, the glow of need starting to swell and uncoil inside her.

"And to finish the trail of fragrances, you have a touch of Black Calla right under your jaw." He shifted upward and buried his face there.

"I was in the mood for something black," she said, gasping when his lips sucked gently on her pulse.

"And that's where I come in, right?" He lifted his head, revealing a cocky grin.

She found herself grinning, admiring his lovely black skin. "Sure enough."

She detected the subtle scent of Sandalwood Musk on his shoulder, and when she leaned up to sniff, she caught a glimpse of the coffee table where the lid of the sample pack lay wide open, with all the miniature bottles of lotion spread out in little groups.

"You've been busy," she noted.

His eyes twinkled. "I have."

Yes, he had. She could smell the myriad of fragrances in the air and, among them, the unmistakable aroma of . . .

"Pizza?"

"I saved you some."

"Let me, um, clean myself up a little and we can pick up where we left off."

She escaped to the bathroom, aware that he was on the verge of pinning her down. She would've let him, too. She took a quick shower and brushed her teeth with the complimentary set in the bathroom.

When she returned, he was reading the labels of one of the bottles again, frowning studiously as if to memorize the ingredients. Tanika grabbed a slice of pizza and took a big bite, smiling sheepishly when her belly growled with hunger.

She strolled over, then settled on his lap, facing

him, forcing him to set the lotion aside and focus on her parted robe. His stirring erection was warm against her skin.

"So, you've become an expert on the lotions, huh?" she said, pretending she hadn't noticed.

Her nipples were tightened, pushing against the parted robe. His gaze followed it down, to where her position held her thighs open, perfectly framing the trim of her nether curls and hints of her labia.

"Not an expert yet, but I will be."

"Of that, I have no doubt. Not as good as me, though."

The dimple appeared on his cheek again. "Oh, yeah? Can you guess what I'm wearing?"

"That's easy. One sexy woman with great legs."

"Damn, you *are* good."

"I get better."

He tipped his head. "I am but a mere student, eager to learn."

She smirked to keep from laughing. "I eat students like you for breakfast."

She felt the nudge of his cock rising. "Not yet you haven't," he said.

"It's not yet breakfast," she pointed out.

She took another bite and chewed, watching him watching her. He took a sip from his wine glass, then handed it to her. She sipped and handed it back.

"Let's see. You're wearing sandalwood on your shoulders, but there are several other scents, mostly on your fingertips, from handling all the bottles."

Having said that, she licked the pizza sauce off her fingertips.

"More pizza?" he asked conversationally, handing her the wine glass again.

She took another sip. "Maybe later, thank you." Wine and pizza. Yum. A man after her own heart. She stopped mid-sip, realizing she'd almost said the last part aloud.

He shifted beneath her, deliberately forcing her to open her thighs wider. Even after the shower, the scent of renewing sex was undeniable. She swallowed audibly.

"Tell me about plum," he said, his hands sliding up her thighs, his thumbs cresting the intersection and hovering, barely touching the folds of her sex, back and forth . . . back and forth . . .

"Plum," he reminded her, leaning forward and nipping gently on her left nipple.

The contact of his teeth on her nipple broke the trance and she released the breath she hadn't realized she'd been holding.

"Purple," she gushed. "Plum. Semitart." Like wine.

"Warming lubricant."

"Yes."

His thumbs came together over her clit, and she watched the fascination on his face as he rubbed in tentative circles, the bloom of arousal drawing the nub. His own erection was becoming more insistent.

"Do you like plum?" he asked, still moving the

pads of his thumb over, around, and barely under her
clitoris.

"Yes."

"It's like the color of your nipples," he said, then
began sucking on one. His tongue swirled and
lapped at the mild pain the edge of his teeth induced.

"Lovely color," he whispered.

"Mmm . . ." How on earth did he do that thing
with his mouth!

He kissed and nuzzled her breasts, nipping, licking, while his fingers rubbed and caressed her flesh
as it grew wetter.

"Grab the plum lube." His husky command had
to be repeated before she reacted.

"Take three droplets and rub it on your nipples."

She did as instructed, fumbling with the bottle
every time his thumbs came together to rub and tug
at her clit. She rubbed the delicate oil over her nipple, feeling the heat occur almost instantly.

"Put it in my—"

She leaned forward, pushing her breast into his
mouth, moaning and arching when he suckled
it hard.

"Oh . . . Damon . . ."

She clutched her other breast with one hand and
the lotion in the other. He laved the soft mound,
then suddenly turned to her clasped breast, nuzzling
her fingers aside and taking it into his mouth for the
same treatment.

"God . . . Umm . . ."

His fingers kept stroking her, drawing on the wetness that now dripped onto his groin.

In the blink of an eye, he'd shifted her, pushing her slightly away from him to slide his thick erection neatly into her wet passage. And just like last time, she was overwhelmed by the fullness of him, of the depth of him. And just like last time, the ribbed sensation of the condom was enough to make her stutter. "G-G-God."

It felt like an eternity before she could look away from him, from the desire in his eyes that damn near burned.

"Rub some plum on your pussy for me."

She'd forgotten that she even held the bottle. There was no point in measuring after her unsteady hand drizzled too much, causing it to spill down his abdomen. She set the bottle aside, afraid she'd upend it entirely, then did as he'd instructed and rubbed it on herself.

His breathing grew rougher as he watched her fingers work, running her fingers at the seam of their union, where her labia was stretched wide to accommodate his cock. She stroked herself, almost masturbating, the mild heat and the scent of plum too much for her not to roll her hips and start the rhythm of sex.

He fingered the oil that remained on his abdomen and his fingers joined hers, slick and hot, his eyes holding hers with their seductive mischief.

"Don't come yet . . . not yet . . ."

He held her down hard, and sucked on her breasts, flexing his hips every now and then in deep strokes.

Tanika tugged his head back and kissed him, tasting wine and plum and more.

"Give it to me now," she demanded.

He nipped her bottom lip, his hands covering her butt and squeezing. "Only when I'm ready."

"You're ready!" Lord knew she was! "Please!"

He brushed her lips with a butterfly kiss, his eyes still holding her captive. "You may eat students like me for breakfast, but right now, I want to show you what I know about eating."

He tugged her upward to a kneeling position, his mouth directly under her gleaming wet sex.

"You smell so goddamned good," he murmured before delving in for the oral tongue lashing.

Tanika gripped the back of the couch, caught between rocking against that clever, hungry mouth of his or hyperventilating . . . or both. She was unprepared for the sudden grasp of his hands on her buttocks as he pulled her closer still, his nose and lips stroking her clit while his tongue delved, licked and flicked in and out of her as if she were made out of plum ice cream.

When he had her delicately writhing on his face, he stroked two fingers into her vagina, searching for and finding the magical spot that pushed her higher, stroking and pumping until the end was inevitable.

Tanika came, crumbling over him, blind and breathless, dizzy and drowning in the surreal aftermath.

She felt weightless as he shifted her down, lowering her onto another ribbed condom covering his rock-hard erection. He kissed her hair, then his mouth, tasting of plum and sex and wine, took hers like a man possessed. He seemed to be everywhere at once, hands and mouth and cock, rocking to a rhythm that brought them closer than skin allowed.

She cupped his head in her hands, feeling the hot escape of his semen, kissing his lips when his arms tightened around her like iron bands.

The broken sounds from him were like additional caresses.

His arms loosened by degrees, and she rested her head against his shoulder, knowing without a doubt that it hadn't been a fluke.

In one night, this man—this well-endowed, sexy geek!—had given her the best orgasms of her life.

I sure could go for a hot, steamy bath," she mumbled, when the cold started to settle on her skin. "Want to?"

"Mmm. I don't take baths."

She tilted her head up and saw he was serious. "How could you not?"

He shrugged. "Takes too much time. I'd rather take a shower, or if I need anything hotter, I'll step into the sauna."

She pushed away from him a bit, his cock limp but still inside her. "I suppose you don't do massages, either?"

"Exercise—and sex—relieve most of my stress."

She resisted tracing the angular planes of his face. "Would it be a far-off guess to say that you don't sleep naked, either?"

That made him look a little chagrined. "I prefer to sleep in my boxer shorts. What's wrong with that?"

"Nothing." But she smiled. At least her instincts about his personality had been right in some areas. "So, you've never dealt with fur-lined handcuffs or velvet ropes?"

This time he raised both eyebrows, waited a couple of seconds, then answered, "A gentleman doesn't kiss and tell."

"Which is as good as a no."

"I'll let you jump to whatever conclusions you want."

"Are you open to the idea?"

He rubbed his jaw. "The interesting thing about submission is the juxtaposition between physical strength, convenient restraints, and mental submissiveness."

Man, he was sure cute when he started throwing around those fifty-dollar words! "It's a simple yes or no, Damon. Would you enjoy restraints?"

He sighed. "Does this line of questioning end with me delving into more ND products?"

She chuckled, kissing him briefly on the lips. "It's my mission in life to see you delve, delve, delve. But right now, I'm dying for a bath, so come on."

"A shower would be—"

"A bath! No ifs, ands, or buts. Let's go!"

Damon eased farther into the bubble-filled tub and sighed, enjoying the sensuous feel of Tanika's body against his chest and the luxury of hot water surrounding them.

"Now, isn't this better than a shower?" she asked.

He wasn't ready to concede. "I'm still in delving mode," he said, referring to the ND bathing salts she'd lavishly poured into the bathwater.

She did a silky flip in the water so that she faced him, her belly sliding over his. "I won't accept that answer when I give you a massage."

"After sitting in this, I won't need a massage," he countered, grabbing her butt and rubbing her soft skin. Her mouth looked so damned kissable. "What is this bubble bath called anyway?"

"Ocean Breeze. It's very, very mild."

He leaned forward, but held back on the kiss he wanted. "Thank God it's not girly."

She smirked. "Aha! A perfect advertising slogan. We should use that on the next ads."

The steam was already working on some of the hair framing her face, bringing out the natural corkscrew curls. A couple of droplets clung to the ends, making her look naïve and youthful, a complete opposite from the sophisticated woman in that glimmering pink gown.

"You know, we do have a unisex line of products," she pointed out. "Un-girly stuff."

"Yeah, I noticed that in the ND Zone Theory diagram. Along with daywear, nightwear, springwear, fallwear, summerwear . . . Anywhere. Seems a bit much to me."

"That's because you've probably used the same classic cologne and aftershave for years."

Not years, exactly. "I stick with what works."

"Not that I mind. You have good taste."

"Thank you . . . I think."

"My point being that in the summer, the body's reaction to heat can change the composition of perfume or cologne, did you know that? Cool weather does the same thing. And depending on where our customers live and the flowers that bloom there, one perfume may be more favorable than another. Even from day to night, the scent may change entirely, or fade completely."

He placed a finger over her lips. "I don't think I can handle a lesson in Fragrances 101 this late in the night."

She licked it, jolting his sex drive a couple of notches higher. "But, Damon, I had a pop quiz all planned out. If you pass, you get a treat. If you fail, I get a treat."

"I'll cram for it. I'm good at cramming."

She rubbed against his groin, causing him to hold his breath at the pleasure. "I've noticed."

He returned the move, but the bathwater sloshed a little too close to the rim of the tub.

"Careful," she said huskily.

He pulled her up his chest so he could kiss her, then on the way down, he coaxed her legs apart and nudged his erection between the folds of her vagina.

"Yes, we wouldn't want to spill," he repeated. "Think you can handle that?"

"Damn straight." She licked her lips, her eyes dark with desire, her ample wet breasts gleaming like caramel. "Come on, big guy, give it to me."

"Nice and slow."

"Aww, damn . . ."

Half an hour later, steam still suspended lazily in the air, their breaths were ragged, and several towels ended up on the floor beside the tub, all soaking wet.

chapter 5

Damon parked his car in the reserved parking spot and stepped out, trying to shake off the unreasonable and inexplicable emotions that had erupted within him the moment he'd woken up alone in the hotel.

The bedsheets had been tangled around his hips, and the pillow next to him still held the scents of Tanika. The indentation on the pillow where she'd slept taunted him. But other than that, there was no trace of her in the room.

Oh, yes. There was the scribbled note: "Lovely night. Have to run. See you at work."

And for the first time in as long as he could remember, he was late to work. He bypassed the elevators in favor of the stairs, taking them two at a time, trench coat and briefcase in hand.

Okay, he wanted to see her. And part of him wanted to kiss her until she felt faint and horny. The other part wanted to remain cool, and, if necessary, retain some distance to give him control.

It was going to be hard to pretend that leaving a

lover's bed without his noticing wasn't bad day-after etiquette. Hadn't he distinctly said he didn't do just one-nighters?

He reached the office and stepped inside, nodding toward the receptionist, then his secretary. His grandmother was already waiting in his office.

"You're late."

"Six minutes."

"Ten, to be precise."

"Good morning to you too, Nana." He kissed her cheek and placed his briefcase and coat on a nearby chair, then made a beeline to the eye-opening coffee, vowing to give his secretary a raise for anticipating his daily routine.

Tanika walked by and abruptly stopped by the door, looking up from some papers she had in her hand, obviously deep in thought. "Mrs. Becker, the new mannequins are in and—"

"Good morning, Ms. Davis," he interrupted.

She looked at him then, a quick flash of sultry recognition in her eyes. "Good morning," she acknowledged with a nod.

Man, he'd badly wanted to hear those words from her, first thing in the morning, naked in bed, instead of greeting her so formally over his cup of coffee while his grandmother watched. He crushed the wayward emotion and dragged his gaze back to his grandmother.

"Mannequins?" he asked, inviting himself into the conversation.

"For the displays. We'll time it with the ad campaigns."

"I see." Damon took another gulp of coffee, struggling with the irrational urge to pick a fight.

His grandmother was back to signing documents and sliding them into his in-box. "Have the giveaway sample gift packs arrived yet?"

Tanika briefly peered at him over her paperwork. "Yes. The online promo stats have come in and . . ."

Her words flowed in a stream of explanations while he watched her lips move, trying not to be sucker-punched by memories of her luscious mouth working his body. Why had she left without a word? Had she become bored already?

". . . I'd say that with that success rate, we're off to a good start, don't you agree, Damon?"

Huh? "Yes, of course."

His grandmother's eyes narrowed. "Excellent. Then the Broadway store will be the first pilot for the men's ND items."

Oh, crap. Is that what he'd just agreed to?

Tanika's eyes twinkled and for a moment he forgot everything but the feel of her body on his in the bathtub, and the way she'd said his name, so wicked and sinful . . .

"I'm glad you're open to the idea, Damon. Finish up your coffee and meet us in the conference room," his grandmother said, before wandering off with Tanika.

Damon stared into the steam of his coffee, trying

to steer his thoughts away from Tanika in bed and back into business.

After the meeting, his grandmother made her way back into his office, dumping more folders on his desk. "Something about you is different today."

"I feel rested. You should try it sometime."

"You keep getting sassier and sassier," she said, trying to hide her amusement behind a scowl.

"It's in the genes."

She harrumphed, but the sound faded abruptly and her hand went absently to her chest. Damon felt a moment of stark panic and popped out of his chair, standing beside her before she knew it. "Chest pains?"

"No!" She batted the air as if his words were pesky flies, then fussed with his tie instead of immediately looking him in the eyes. "I'm just fine. Just following doctor's orders to get some rest. Do you think you can handle these reports?"

"Yes."

"Thank you, sweetie. I'll put in a couple of hours, then leave around noon—"

"You should leave now." He tried to escort her to the door.

"Stop it," she admonished gently. "I get enough smothering from my doctor. I'm strong enough to work a couple more hours and I don't intend to go home a second sooner. You should know better by now."

"Yes'm."

She harrumphed again and handed him the reports, a devious gleam in her eyes. "Get to work."

"I'm calling Dr. Wagner," he said, referring to the family doctor.

"You will do no such thing."

He planted a kiss on her forehead and grabbed the reports. "I could be convinced not to if you promise to go home early."

"Damon Alexander Becker, don't you threaten me. It's talk like that that gives me chest pains."

Jesus!

"Now, come on, don't give me that look," she said as she headed toward the door. "I love you, too. Just stop hovering, okay?"

He gave her a hug, his heart keeping his worry mute.

"Okay, okay," she conceded. "I'll call Dr. Wagner."

"Thanks."

But even after she left, concern churned in his gut.

Tanika was locked up in other meetings for most of the morning, but it didn't keep thoughts of Damon from intruding.

She tried to force her thoughts back to business, but at one point, she'd been so caught up in the memory of the night before that the phantom thrust of his erection seemed to ride between her thighs and rock right into her womb.

She'd managed to stifle her pleasure-gasp with a cough, then crossed her legs and casually buttoned up her jacket.

It had been tough enough to leave him in the morning. He'd looked all spent and handsome among the sheets; it had been all she could do not to wake him up with a kiss on the lips.

Staying would've sent the wrong message, though. But it had been so tempting.

Nope, she made the rules, so she ought to stick by them.

Deciding to take a firm stand on their new relationship, she'd reluctantly sneaked out, leaving behind a note that had taken her almost fifteen minutes to put together.

Tanika expected to have the relationship under control and in perspective, but when he'd greeted her this morning, she knew she was in trouble. He was just as potent in a three-piece suit as he was naked and moving against her.

Christ Almighty . . .

The day chugged along and finally she returned to her office, spending the next hour going through her e-mails, stalling on the one from Damon stating:

Please deliver the detailed report of the summary you distributed in the meeting. I'd like to have it by five o'clock if possible.

Her finger hovered over the keyboard as she glared at the message for a moment, then she typed, "Do you want it on your desk by the end of the day?"

Ha, take that. She hoped he remembered the reference to the ad she'd mocked up.

Less than two minutes later, her computer popped up with a timestamp to let her know he'd read her message. But as the minutes slipped by, he did not respond.

Perhaps Damon Becker the businessman was just entirely too stuffy to respond to something like that while at work. It figured. She much preferred the demanding lover he could be instead.

Would it kill him to reply to her e-mail?

"Whatever." With a huff, she turned her back on the machine and went to work on other things, but she kept glancing at the clock as four o'clock became four-thirty and then five o'clock.

With two minutes to spare, she printed out the detailed report he'd requested and set it up in a binder. The office was like a ghost town, with everyone either heading out the door or already gone.

Tanika walked down the long hall to Damon's office and knocked before stepping inside. The butterflies in her stomach fluttered when she spotted him leaning against his desk, his shirtsleeves rolled up, revealing his muscular forearms.

He deliberately glanced down at his watch, then back at her. "In the nick of time."

"Excuse me?"

"I hope you don't make it a habit to be tardy with requested reports, Ms. Davis."

Her temper now fully ignited, she coolly placed the report in his in-box and turned to leave. But he spun her around, closing the door in the process and trapping her against the wall, where he crushed his mouth against hers in a hungry, unexpected kiss.

Trying to say his name only allowed his mouth more access to hers. She bit his bottom lip softly, but he bit her back, causing her anger to steadily succumb into desire. Man, he was changing before her eyes, like a superhero, transforming from staunch businessman to ardent lover.

He tasted of mint, felt like hard muscle, and smelled like heaven. She wrapped her arms around him and simply allowed herself to indulge in the moment.

When she was limp and mindless, they broke for air, letting their hard breaths speak for themselves. Words seemed inadequate and unnecessary, and even as logical thought started to return, she smiled up at Damon.

"You set me up," she murmured. "You knew I'd storm in here."

His smile appeared, slow as a sunrise. "I didn't think it'd be that easy."

Somewhere outside the office, she could hear doors closing as people left the building. The sounds matched the bump of her heart when his hands moved under her jacket and closed over her breasts.

His hands continued their caresses. "Think we can manage before the janitor arrives?"

"Mr. Becker!" she said in mock surprise.

"Call me Damon." Then lifting her up, he moved her onto his desk.

"Wait," she protested. "Lock the door."

"I did."

Sure enough, he had.

"I'm fascinated by this Mandarin Magic," he said, even as he carefully undid the buttons of her shirt. "I've been wondering what it would taste like against your breasts."

He worked evenly, letting the tension build as he went from one button to the next, revealing her black lace bra. It was more arousing to hear his breathing become deeper still, his gaze focused on her dark, aroused nipples against the lace.

"If you want to keep your underwear intact, you'd better take it off now, otherwise I can't be held responsible," he warned.

She knew they were about to reenact the ad she'd done for the photo shoot. Except now she didn't give a damn about artistic creativity. Now all she wanted was Damon.

Removing the underwear was an erotic experience in itself. Their bodies were so close, that when she shimmied the thong off, she rubbed against the erection straining in his trousers.

She'd barely kicked it off before he began running his hands up her legs, pushing her sensible knee-high business skirt to her thighs.

"And another thing," he said, holding her gaze as he unzipped his trousers, shucked his underwear down, and worked his condom on. "Next time, wake me before you leave."

Because she felt guilty about it still, she kissed him instead of replying, then groaned in the middle of the kiss when he lifted her to the edge of his desk, pushed her legs apart, and thrust two fingers probingly into her sensitive sex. They slid in easily as she was still slick from being half-aroused all day.

He stroked her deeply, slowly, tasting her mouth to the same rhythm as his hand movements.

"So hot," he whispered. "You look so good this way."

Hopelessly mesmerized by his confession, she could do nothing but hold on while he explored her again. "No fair . . ."

He slanted his mouth over hers, sucking gently on her lips, tonguing her when she parted her mouth again.

"Gimme more," she pleaded.

He smiled faintly. "Like this?"

There was a faint hum of sound and she glanced down in time to see that he'd slid on the Cock Clinger. The elastic cock ring was snug at the base of his erection, the small clit stimulator shaking in a tiny anemone frenzy.

"Delve with me," he murmured, then replacing the touch of his fingers with the blunt tip of his erection, he slid thick and firm into her until he was wedged to the hilt.

The tight fit and the humming vibrations against her clit almost rocked her off the desk. The first tremors started deep inside her, anticipating another thrust. Except it didn't come.

"Now. More!"

"Patience," Damon said, sounding like he also needed a good dose. He leaned her back a bit. "I still want to taste your breasts."

The front clasp of her bra was worked apart, with his erection still throbbing within her, her breath hitching with the growing humming against her aching clit.

Damon began to place drops of the cool mandarin-scented lotion on her bare breasts.

With circular caresses, he worked the lotion into her skin, his palms slick and yet abrading against her nipples. His hungry, nipping mouth followed, and before long, she found herself moaning, muttering curses, and locking her legs around his hips, rocking against him for completion.

His hands and mouth moved over her skin, teasing the sensitive mandarin-scented flesh, moisturizing her skin with the lotion. The pleasure was intense, cresting toward unbearable, and she quietly moaned his name.

Damon murmured a soft unintelligible word, his

mouth hovering over her nipple. Then he suckled and worked his mouth over and over again until every part of her breast was aching and full.

He made his way up her neck, nibbling and nuzzling her under her jaw, then covering her mouth with a devouring kiss that tasted of lust and lotion.

His hips responded, rolling back like a fine-tuned piston engaging, straining into her with the slow promise of full-blown intensity. The starched cotton of his shirt felt almost grainy against her sensitive nipples and the world seemed to recede around her as her whole being focused on the sensation of him inside her, enhanced by the humming Cock Clinger.

Tanika felt shaky, breathless, and the spiking fever of desire kept growing hotter. As much as she wanted to move, too, he wouldn't let her, and found herself surrendering to the overwhelming desire, felt herself dragged under in it, with him at the reins.

"Oh, God . . . God . . ." Tanika moaned weakly, desperately wanting more motion, more rhythm, grinding as she pushed against his grip to get more.

Damon muttered something gruff and hot, but she couldn't make out the words, only their meaning. His thrusts remained ruthlessly slow, but somehow deeper. The humming tickles against her clit were creaming her inside, making her vagina feel like a wet mouth, sucking, sucking.

"Fuck!" The lash of passion finally gripped inside her hard, like a fist over glass, clenching in her womb and tingling all the way to where the Cock Clinger sealed her body to his.

She came undone, biting Damon's shirt to stifle the scream. Tremors washed over her, cresting and rippling slowly until they faded like lapping water.

With a rigid thrust, Damon's hot ejaculation followed, his arms embracing her fiercely as his ejaculation spilled inside her.

The steady hum of the cock ring wrung the orgasm out of every nerve ending, until she felt semi-electrocuted. Still grunting, Damon reached down and turned it off, then clung to her as if he were also having trouble staying upright.

The world returned, bringing with it walls and chairs and the hard desk she sat on. In the silence of the room, their recovering breaths seemed too loud, her body too sweaty. She suddenly wished for a bed to crawl into with him, to pull bedsheets over their heads and sleep off the delicious aftermath.

Damon tipped her head back and kissed her, tenderly, taking his time.

She cupped his head in her hands and kissed him back, and eventually the mesh of lips ended in soft butterfly touches. Her lips felt swollen and overly soft, and each little kiss he planted on hers made her heart ache in a way that was oddly nonsexual and infinitely precious. It was something more than desire, more than the intimacy of physical pleasure. Certainly more than just casual sex.

Christ, what was she doing?

A spear of panic snaked up her spine and she knew she had to put some distance between them soon. Pushing at his chest, she broke the contact, unable to look him in the eyes right away.

"That was a wonderful surprise. Not bad for half an hour, huh?" she said brightly, dropping her legs from around his hips. "But we should probably get out of here before we hear the janitor's vacuum being dragged down the hall."

The switch of mood was instantaneous. Damon tensed without moving a muscle. When she shifted, he nonetheless pulled out of her sensitive sex, his cock limp and wet from the copulation, the Cock Clinger looking right at home. Damon took a few steps back and began to wordlessly straighten his clothing.

She could feel his gaze on her thighs and breasts, so she stood on her weakened legs, turned her back on him and adjusted her skirt and bra. The damned buttons of her shirt seemed to have a mind of their own and new emotions had sprung into her chest that had no business being there. And, Lord, would her snatch ever stop purring? No wonder men called it "pussy."

She heard his zipper close, then silence. Her fingers fumbled and a damned button popped out again. His hands settled on her hips and he turned her, pushing her fingers aside and taking over the task.

"What happened?" he murmured. "Got more than you'd bargained for?"

The panic she'd been trying to deny bloomed, and for a second, she was tempted to run out the door. Instead she forced a smile and stayed rooted to the spot. "What do you mean? Don't you normally last more than five minutes?"

"I'm not talking about my endurance and you know it."

As he buttoned her shirt, she tried to ignore the feel of his knuckles and fingertips methodically hiding her cleavage. Finally, she looked into deep brown eyes, feeling more naked as he steadily looked back as if he could see all her scrambling thoughts.

"I'm just ready to roll out of here, that's all," she lied.

He waited a heartbeat. "I suppose so."

He turned and walked around the desk to get his briefcase, the movement of air reawakening the scent of mandarin lotion and fresh sex.

Heaven help her, she was never going to be able to use that lotion again.

Desperate to get out of there, she unlocked the door and, from the corner of her eye, saw him lean down, grab her flimsy thong off the carpet and shove it in his pocket.

"Oops, wouldn't want to forget that," she said, stretching out her hand for it.

Damon shook his head. "Finders keepers."

"Come on, seriously." She wiggled her fingers.

A forced smile touched his lips as he moved past her. "Next time don't wear anything at all."

There won't be a next time!

Frustrated, she bit her lip to keep from voicing the retort and instead said, "Fine. Keep it. I need to use the ladies' room."

She turned the corner and hurried to the restroom to clean herself up as best she could. When she finally went to the sink, she turned the cold water knob and held her wrists underneath the flow.

The reflection in the mirror made her look a little distraught. Her nipples were still tight against her shirt and her lips were definitely puffy. The nipples were easy to hide under her jacket, but her lips declared to the world that she'd been recently kissed and kissed well. Kissed and fucked. God, it had been so good!

Kisses, she could deal with. In fact, she didn't mind his hard kisses at all. It was his soft kisses that had her stressing out. It made her feel . . . too much.

Hell, she was probably making a big deal out of nothing.

With that in mind, she barged out of the ladies' room and found Damon waiting for her. Forcing that fake smile back on her face, she followed him to the elevators where it seemed to take forever for the elevator to arrive.

Once they were inside and descending, she realized there was no music to break the tension. She turned to him, unable to take the silence any longer. "Once you see the report I dropped off, you'll see why thongs will bring more sales than socks. And since you kept *my* thong, that should speak for itself. I mean, I doubt you would've asked for my socks, right?"

"I've never seen you in socks. Maybe I'd find them sexy and want to keep them, too," he replied.

"We could try that angle," she conceded, "but I doubt it will make a salable point at the next meeting."

A muscle immediately jerked in his jaw and his eyes darkened several hues.

"Are you trying to make your business arguments by using sex?" His voice, she noticed, dropped just a few dangerous degrees when he was really ticked.

"Just making conversation."

"Do you think sex would sway my decision in business?"

"Don't be insulting. I was just asking—"

The elevator doors opened but he ignored them, instead standing between her and the only escape.

"As good as you are, I don't base my business decisions on sex. If you want a whore, go find someone else. If you want a lover, I suggest you tread very carefully." If possible, his voice had lowered even more. He took the thong out of his pocket and deliberately placed it in her hand.

When the doors started to close, he held them open and stepped aside.

Embarrassed, she shoved the thong into her purse and walked past him. "You are blowing things out of proportion."

"Am I?" It was bad enough that she couldn't tell if he was being sarcastic or not.

He pulled his car keys out of his pocket. "I know sex is a sport for you, Tanika, but don't try to use me."

He was halfway to the building doors before she caught up to him, the need to apologize burning a hole in her. "I'm sorry."

He studied her for an uncomfortably long moment, then he nodded, his eyes still hard with a don't-pull-that-shit-on-me-again look.

"I didn't mean to give you that impression, Damon."

He nodded, but his expression remained the same. "Okay."

They reached the door and he held it open. "Apology accepted."

"Thank you."

A full second rolled by before he exhaled. "Want to come over tonight? I'll make dinner."

The panic returned like a shark circling closer. "I can't. I promised to visit my sister and her newborn son."

His expression softened. "Okay."

After awkward goodbyes, they went to their cars, parked as they were days before, side by side, his severe and hers sporty.

He had just started the engine of his car when she hurried over, not wanting the day to end on a bad note.

He lowered the window and she discreetly reached into her purse, pulled out the thong, and dropped it into his lap. "Finders keepers."

She winked and left before he could respond.

chapter 6

Visiting her sister Cindy always meant Tanika would leave smelling like baby powder, having eaten too much, and inevitably, carrying some leftovers home.

It never failed to amaze Tanika how Cindy looked so obnoxiously happy with baby spittle on her fashionable shirt and her hair rioting from fashion neglect. More amazing was that her husband hardly seemed to notice. Tanika chose to believe that they'd both lost a bit of their minds to their adorable chubby baby they'd nicknamed Bubba.

"So, how's the business end of things?" Cindy asked, as if she hadn't called to grill her several times a day.

"It's all under control," Tanika replied, chucking the baby gently under his double chin.

"And what about Mr. Starchy Suit?"

"Damon? He got a little bent out of shape when we explained that thongs were now replacing socks in the display area."

Cindy chuckled. "So it's 'Damon' now?"

"I have to work with him on the marketing ideas. Keeping the formality gets old, especially when we're talking bras and negligees."

"I tell you, I can hardly wait to meet that man. He sounds so uptight."

Tanika shrugged. "He's the epitome of Becker products. Cut. Tight. And impeccable."

"It's actually the perfect contrast for our products."

"Only you would think so."

"Of course." The baby squirmed and Cindy held him out. "Here, you wanna hold him?"

Before Tanika could object, Cindy had placed Bubba on her shoulder, and Tanika automatically handled the child like hot glass. "Girl, you know I don't do babies!"

Her sister dismissed the remark. "Just tap him on the back. He needs to burp."

"Jesus, Cin," Tanika muttered, doing as instructed.

"Get used to it. I intend to have you babysit."

"If you're trying to scare me, it's working."

Cindy sighed and slouched into her seat, smiling serenely. "So, you and Damon aren't fighting, are you?"

"We have our differences of opinion. I mean, the fact that he'd pick socks over thongs says it all."

"Sounds like a guy who would rather play it safe than take risks. Maybe that's why he's running this project," Cindy observed.

Tanika peeked at Bubba and found him staring at her with a drooly, slack-jawed look. Sure, he smelled like cookies and looked incredibly huggable, but the fact that he was waiting to burp was like a ticking bomb.

"How's Mrs. Becker?" Cindy asked.

"The grandmother looks great, and I've seen her use the sick card every now and then, but she sure is sharp as a whip."

Bubba gurgled loudly, and like a supermom, Cindy whipped out a wipe rag and dabbed at the dribbling milk.

"No need to cringe like that," Cindy reprimanded. "He didn't get any on your shirt."

"I don't know if I'm cut out for this."

Her sister chuckled as she completed the task. "Sure you are. But first you need a man who'll plan to stick around."

"Geez. I hate when you do that. Please don't start with the lectures. I'm still sowing my oats."

"Sowing your oats?" Cindy's gaze softened. "That business with Leroy still messing with your mind?"

"I learned from my mistakes," Tanika snapped, "I won't make a fool of myself giving every last bit of my heart and soul to my next lover. It's now officially proprietary. Mine and mine alone. From here on out, all I'm ever giving any man is just sex."

"Damn, Nika. Leroy broke your heart, but—I'm telling you this because I love you—he wasn't worth the heartache, sis. And you're going to make a bigger mistake if you think sex is what will make you happy."

"I don't. I'm not."

"Well, sleeping with every man you meet is not going to make you happy."

"What the— Who says I'm sleeping with every man I meet? And if I do, isn't that my business?"

"Nika, You're shortchanging yourself with this casual sex! Really, I know you see that it can get dangerous."

Tanika risked a hand away from the baby to gesture in frustration. "I'm a big girl, Cindy. So what? More importantly, why are we even discussing this?"

Cindy looked like she was about to launch into another lecture, but Tanika headed her off. "I think your boy is about to do his thing again."

Cindy wiped at the drool and shook her head, muttering to herself. "Let me get the bassinette. I'll be right back."

Thankful that the conversation was at least temporarily closed, Tanika looked down just as Bubba snuggled closer, sleepy-eyed and flashing the sweetest smile she'd seen on his lips. His head of delicate corkscrew curls and his smooth, plump mocha skin were so soft.

When Tanika looked up, Cindy was standing by the doorway, grinning like a cat that swallowed a canary.

"If you start now," Cindy said, "they could start kindergarten together."

"They who?"

"Your baby and Bubba. Maybe your current lover won't mind making a sperm donation."

Tanika groaned. "My ovaries just shriveled up. I don't even know if I'm ready to be a godparent, much less become a mother."

"Excuses, excuses. Your clock's a-ticking, you know?"

"Cindy!"

"Okay! All right. I'm shutting up already."

But her arms felt a little empty after she placed Bubba in his bassinette.

Later, as Tanika drove home, she mentally replayed the torrid heartache after Leroy had broken up with her. Even now, the memory of it was a sensitive bruise, still carrying some self-pity and keen humiliation.

God, she'd *loved* him! In fact, she'd been so blind with love, she'd gone right ahead and built daydreams around a future with him. In return, her declaration had ended with his priceless, stunned expression of panic that had instantly shattered her heart. Worse was when he'd fumbled through his tired lines that even then had sounded far more desperate than sincere.

It's not you, it's me . . .

You'll find love again, baby . . .

I just need something different, something more . . .

Well, so did she.

She had a career to focus on and right now she was footloose and fancy-free. As the saying went, the world was like one big friggin' oyster. And Damon was just the key to all the liberating fun she wanted to have.

With the window down, the dark cityscape rolled by in a cool blur and Tanika sighed, running a hand over her custom haircut.

God as her witness, she was steering clear of anything resembling love this time around.

The following morning, Damon found himself staring at his computer while mentally trying to solve the puzzle that was Tanika. He sipped coffee and leaned closer to study the numbers on a spreadsheet, then ran them twice again against different data. Okay, so maybe his grandmother was risking part of the company's reputation, but the numbers all but guaranteed a profit.

He flipped to another spreadsheet and sipped more coffee. If only she were as easy to run as the numbers before him. And what the hell kind of a move was it to drop the thong in his lap?

If he ran into her at the copier, was he supposed to "excuse me, pardon me" his way around her? As if he hadn't once tasted the honey of her vagina trembling against his tongue? As if she hadn't had to bite back his name in the midst of an orgasm? As if, as if, as if . . .

Shit.

He pushed back from his desk and went to look out the window, determined to get his mind straight. It wasn't as if she'd moved the relationship to this point on her own. There had to be a compromise between her need for uncomplicated sex and his need for some intimacy.

Somewhere along the line, he knew he wasn't going to settle for less.

Heaving out an exhale, he returned to his desk and picked up the phone, determined to keep his mind on business for the rest of the day.

He ended up making and taking more phone calls during the day and was in the middle of listening to a vendor talk about his grandkids when Tanika entered his office, hand-signaling that she could return later.

He signaled that she should take a seat, but she perched on the edge of the chair, then took one of his notepads and scribbled down a note, and handed it to him.

"Want to go to dinner after work?" it said.

Damon's heart did a silly pubescent dance.

"Sure." He nodded.

Tanika stood, gave him an almost shy thumbs-up and left.

In his ear, the voice of the vendor droned on, but Damon could hardly make sense of it. Man, she had him turned around! One minute he wasn't sure if she could make him possibly feel worse, questioning if he was compromising his morals, and the next she had him feeling like a hyperactive sixth-grader with a hot date to the dance.

Tanika checked her wristwatch and noticed she was running about twenty minutes behind. As a last-minute touch-up, she rubbed some vanilla lotion on her hands, cheeks, and neck, then tried to steady the butterflies in her stomach.

When she closed the blinds to her office, she saw Damon patiently waiting downstairs, leaning against his car, as casual and handsome as a model.

Dinner. Just dinner. So why was her stomach a mass of fluttering nerves?

She hurried downstairs, feeling irrationally giddy to see his slow smile for a greeting. Without a word, he opened the passenger door of his car and she stepped inside.

Once he settled into the driver's seat and backed the car out of the parking spot, he asked, "Are you very hungry?"

"Not exactly."

"Mind if I make a brief stop before we find something to eat? A friend of mine is selling his boat and I wanted to take a quick look at it."

"No problem." She glanced at his angled profile, tempted to admire him as he drove. Instead she looked out the window. "Boat, huh?"

He shrugged and smoothly shifted the car into gear. "I've liked boats since I was a kid."

The image of him as a child was impossible to conjure. "Is it a large boat?"

"No. Not quite."

That could mean anything, like it held a kitchen but not a suite of bedrooms. Or it was a mini-yacht rather than a mondo-yacht, if there was such a thing.

"Do you have any hobbies?" he asked after a while.

She hesitated. "I, ah . . . not really."

He chuckled briefly, the deep rumble drawing her gaze back to him. "Other than sex, there must be things you do for fun."

"Well, sure. I play pool, enjoy a good game of darts, . . ." She shrugged and looked back out her window. "And sometimes I knit."

"Knit?"

She could see his grin lingering in the reflection of her window and it caused her to frown. "It's no big deal. Lots of people knit."

"Of course." His smooth agreement was spoken much too innocently.

"Not often. Just a couple of scarves in the winter. Baby blankets. That kind of thing."

"Hmm."

She was tempted to add the ridiculous comment that she specialized in "doilies for dildos" but he'd probably give the same response.

"Speaking of likes, what restaurant would you like to go to?"

"No preference. Did you have anything in mind?"

"Thai?"

"Love Thai."

"Excellent."

The conversation dwindled into a comfortable silence and the mellow music floated between them. Tanika was tempted to ask him several more questions, but stifled the instinct.

She had no long-term designs on him, except for maybe his body. Okay, definitely his body.

In a couple more days, she'd have worked him out of her system—he'd likely work her out of his system, as well—and they could say their goodbyes without any hard feelings between them.

At least, that was the plan.

Tanika was increasingly aware of how pensive and quiet Damon was. He drove as if his thoughts were miles away, but she sensed she had something to do with the severe frown that had ruffled his forehead.

Much too soon, the car crunched over gravel as they neared the gates of the ritzy marina. While the seagulls squawked at one another, the guard reviewed Damon's ID, eyed Tanika through the window, then handed Damon a key followed by some brief directions.

Tanika hadn't expected to end up at what looked like a floating warehouse. The wind was nippy and the planks beneath her feet moaned with the slightest sway of water, but once inside the huge building, the temperature got a little warmer. There was a huge skylight in the middle of the roof, lending glowing light to the interior. It smelled slightly musty, of sea and lumber, the scent reminding her of Damon after vigorous sex and sweat.

The water lapped against the side of the 1950s-looking speedboat.

Well, she had the gleaming chrome and wood right, but the boat was definitely built for speed more than yachtlike leisure. There were no sails, no penny-loafer and crumb-cake nooks on this boat. It might be old, but it was beautifully built, and despite the years, it looked like it still had a powerful engine.

"Sweet, isn't it?" Damon murmured. He ran his hands over the side of the boat, caressing the honey-colored wood, examining the sleek, clean, classic design, stepping inside to peer at the engine.

He was like a kid in a candy store, making little assessing noises as he looked the boat over. A knob on the steering wheel made him grin. A wavy stripe on the side of the chair made him nod, as if answering an unspoken question.

He squatted down next to the control panels and studied each, looking pleased with what he found.

"So, is it all you dreamed it would be?" she asked.

"Oh, yeah." He tore his gaze away from the boat long enough to look at her. "And worth every penny, too."

"I thought you'd go for something more . . . I don't know . . . high-tech? Modern?"

He disembarked and dusted off his hands. "She's the real deal, with lots of authentic parts and lots of character. She doesn't have to roar like a lion and do Mach one."

"She?" Tanika teased.

"Well, yes. She's a classic. Look at that retrofitted hull, these panels . . . And these knobs are the real deal." His sheepish grin was irrepressible.

"You're hot when you talk dirty," she teased. "Come on, say something about the rudder."

He chuckled. "Maybe later I'll whisper some naughty boat-talk to you . . . if you're good."

"Pervert."

"What can I say? I'm a sailor."

His phone chirped and he answered the call. Tanika took a few steps toward the boat, trying to see it through his eyes.

When he finally disconnected the call, he looked entirely too pleased with himself. "It's all done but the signing. He even threw in some scuba gear to boot."

"Nice guy."

"I'll hold my opinion until I see the gear first," he said. "Do you swim?"

He walked past her to a door labeled STORAGE.

"I do a pretty mean dog paddle," she replied. "My body fat pretty much ensures I stay afloat."

He turned the knob, but kept his eyes on her,

looking her over from head to toe, his focus now completely on her. "You don't have to fish for compliments, honey. You know you have a bombshell body. In fact, I wouldn't mind seeing you naked again, bent over . . . waxing my boat."

She coughed up a laugh. "In your dreams!"

He chuckled, tugging her into the smaller room. It too had a skylight, which illuminated oars, ropes, life-saver jackets, and other equipment. It was easy to tell by the coats of dust on the items just how often they were used. Almost to the end of the small room were two shower stalls and four wall lockers. The fresh scent of wood and the gleaming steel of the shower stalls was proof enough that they had been a recent addition.

Tanika looked back at Damon and caught him staring at her, a certain familiar gleam in his eyes. "Is the scuba gear not here?"

"It's probably in the locker," he replied, "but all this talk has given me an idea."

He shoved his hands into his trouser pockets and looked around, obviously planning something.

"What are you up to, Damon?"

"Remember the ad with the shower scene in it?"

Oh, no. Not the one in which she was wearing only a Becker shirt and little more than cold, puckered skin.

"Not a good idea—"

"Oh, it's the perfect idea," he said, shrugging out of his jacket. "Come on, let's do some delving."

"Hold up! Wait just a minute. I thought we were going to dinner?"

"We will."

Once his jacket was off, she saw the bulge of his erection forming in his pants. His lopsided grin told her he was not going to be easily deterred.

"I'll even give you my shirt," he promised, already untucking it.

She crossed her arms. "No way."

"Where's your Naughty Devil spirit?" He kept undressing, using a peg nearby as a makeshift clothes rack. His belt clattered to the ground.

"My sexual fantasy role-playing requires warm places."

He winked. "So do mine. Come on, you know you want to."

She pointed to her surroundings. "It's damp. Cold. I'll freeze to death!"

"No you won't." He worked his shoes and socks off, then dropped his trousers, hanging them on the same hook as his jacket and tie.

"Damon . . ."

"Trust me, you'll be cold on the outside but hot on the inside." His fingers began to unbutton his shirt and she was struck by how handsome and masculine he was.

"No. Absolutely not."

He stepped toward her, holding her hostage with his gaze. "Say yes. Didn't you enjoy last night on the desk? Knowing anyone could come knocking at any moment? Didn't you get a thrill out of that?"

"That was different." But still she didn't move when he leaned down to kiss her. It was, she realized, his goddamned kisses that were so deliciously devastating. He took her mouth in a slow, heated kiss that made her toes curl and her breath hitch. So much for freezing to death . . .

It took a huge chunk of willpower not to run her hands over his chest. He shifted closer still, sliding his hand under her jacket and over her breasts, gently squeezing and molding until she couldn't hold back her hum of pleasure.

"I want you," he murmured, pulling her against him so she'd feel the unmistakable firmness of his erection. "Here in this room. Now."

He kissed her again when she was about to object. His lips moved over hers, sealing each kiss with skillful licks and sucks. "Say yes."

His thumbs found her straining nipples and coaxed them through her lacy bra, angling his head to deepen the kiss. Her womb did a soft melting flip that left her little choice. "If you make it fast, maybe," she finally gasped.

One of his arms went around her, holding her closer as he ground his hips against hers. With his other hand, he sank his fingers into her hair, holding her head back with a gentle firmness so their lips didn't touch. "Not good enough. I want to hear you say yes."

"You're pushing your luck, Mr. Becker," she bluffed, wanting to gain some of the control back.

His lips brushed hers and she nipped his lower lip, smiling when she heard his intake of breath. "Either call me Damon, or call me sir."

"Sir?"

"Mmm. Yeah." He kissed her again, just a brushing tease of his tongue over her lips, then his hands searched her skirt, found the zipper, and seconds later, the skirt slid to the ground.

"Wait, wait . . . this floor is filthy and my clothes—"

"Woman, I'll cover the dry-cleaning. Now take your clothes off." He molded his hands on her buttocks, caressing with a slow circular motion.

Even in the crisp coolness, she could smell everything that was him. His cologne. The elemental scent of his skin. She licked her lips, wanting to taste him.

His nostrils flared and his eyes heated. It was almost overwhelming to have so much desire focused on her.

"For me. Do it," he whispered.

He let her take half a step back, then watched her as the jacket came off, her camisole, bra, and lastly, her thong and shoes.

Yes, the air was cold, but it didn't abate the rush of heat in her veins. And when he removed his underwear, she watched with a watering mouth as his rigid cock sprung free, lancing into the air, so thick and masculine. It barged out from between the bottom of his unbuttoned shirt, making him look disheveled and yet unexpectedly formal.

Damon shrugged out of his shirt, revealing muscled shoulders and a tight chest. Stepping closer to her fallen clothes, he slid his shirt over her shoulders, drawing his lingering warmth against her skin. It fell almost to her thighs, engulfing her like a ghostly embrace.

His hands looked so strong and steady as he drew the material aside like a curtain, brushing the cotton against her tight nipples before exposing them to the chilling air again. His gaze slowly shifted past her breasts, then her tiny navel ring, to the trim strip of her pubic hair.

His cock nudged toward her like an impatient horse pulling at the reins.

"You are so goddamned sexy," he said gruffly.

He looked like he couldn't believe his luck, and that thrilled her even more.

"Is this what you want . . . sir?"

A faint smile appeared on his lips and step by step, he walked her backward into the shower stall. "Darling, you know what I want."

With her back against the cold stainless steel, he moved in for the kiss, his body crushing against hers, skin to skin, lips to lips, his erection lodging hot and heavy between her thighs.

The kiss became more urgent, spiraling out of control, until all she felt was the sheer need to have him inside her, to wrap her legs around his stiff cock and feel him thrusting, driving into her growing, aching wetness until the pleasure stripped her of thought.

"Damon," she moaned, blindly reaching for his cock, holding the smooth, firm flesh in her soft clasp as she stroked him.

It pulsed hotly in her hand, eliciting a groan from Damon that seemed to weaken his knees.

"No!" He pulled her hand away. "I won't last if you do that."

He pushed her feet apart with his, his right hand pushing past her navel and delving between her thighs, past the folds of her labia and deeper still.

"Call me sir," he growled breathlessly in her ear.

For a full minute, she couldn't say a word as his fingers dipped into her vagina, lubricating and rubbing over her sensitive clitoris in turn.

His inquisitive fingertips searched her, roaming the space between her clit and her vagina with just the right pressure to make her leg muscles tremble.

"You . . . Oh. God," she finally gasped, standing on her toes as his fingers thrust deeper.

Damon was relentless, kissing her, nibbling and nuzzling her breasts and neck, doing everything but making her come.

"Damon . . . please . . ." She grasped his cock, trying to bring him to the same level of suffering. Damon froze, thrusting almost against his will and groaning.

Abruptly, his wet fingers covered hers, intending to remove her hold, but she continued to stroke his length. His whispered profanity seared warmly against her cheek, then he pulled away suddenly so that she almost fell to the floor.

"Enough," he managed between breaths. "Wet. I want to see you wet."

She leaned heavily against the wall at her back. "I am."

"Soaking wet."

I am! He reached out and turned the hot water knob. The spray fell from the shower head, landing at her feet with an ice-cold splash.

*D*amon couldn't take his eyes from Tanika's flushed skin, from the desire in her eyes and the invitation of her parted lips.

She shivered a little when the water hit their feet, looking sexier than the ad she'd posed for, but she didn't complain. In fact, her breath hitched.

The air became rich with moisture, and the sounds of water circling down the drain joined their heavy breathing.

Seconds went by and the water slowly became warmer, until steam began to float around them.

Not trusting himself to kiss her, he pushed her gently under the spray of water, watching as his shirt lost all its starch and became translucent and clingy, revealing her dark purplish nipples, the smooth flank of her butt, and even the tattoo of the naughty devil. His cock strained so hard, it hurt.

Closing her eyes, Tanika cupped her breasts, shaping the water as it washed over her body, as if she were alone, modeling only for him. She turned so the spray fell over her neck, wetting the shirt even further, the image burning itself into his mind.

"Touch yourself, babe," Damon said. "Masturbate for me."

Her eyes opened slightly and a blush of self-awareness crept up her neck to her cheeks, accented by the billowing steam.

"Do it, because you already know you can turn me on, because you know how much I really want to see you do it."

She licked the water from her lips, a tiny smile remaining. "Yes, sir."

As the droplets of water fell over her, she slid her hand down between her thighs, parting her legs to show him everything she was doing. The golden chain bracelet on her wrist glistened in the water, her long elegant fingers covered her trimmed mons a second before the red tips of her fingernails slid out of view.

Although her strokes started out a little stilted, she soon eased into her own pleasure, squeezing her breast in one hand and masturbating with the other. The soft wet splashing sound of her hand's rhythmic motion had him reaching for his erection to stroke himself, too.

She moaned, a sound that was less weakness than need, continuing to masturbate for him, peering at him through her lashes, her face slack as her pleasure mounted. She said his name, barely formed the word, and he heard the telltale hitch of her impending orgasm.

He fell to his knees and buried his face between her legs, his tongue delving into her vagina, his mouth sucking on the distended clit between her fingers as he pulled her right leg over his shoulder.

He thrust two, then three fingers into her, licking her flustered clit with each motion, curling his tongue into her honeyed wetness, kissing and stroking with quick, velvety clit licks.

Tanika suddenly bucked under the surge of pleasure, trembling like a flutter of wind-slapped silk beneath his lips while his fingertips were clenched inside her vaginal passage. Her harsh gush of breath was cut off by two sensuous whimpers when he took another kiss from there, wringing out the last of it. Despite her fingers clutching his head, he didn't let up until the tiny little quakes that shook her hips had settled into weak moans.

Damon nuzzled her with a final vaginal kiss, feeling his own orgasm gripping in his testicles, about to rupture.

Almost wild with the need to possess her, he

stood, braced her against the steel wall, and with al-most savage moves, slid hard and rigid into the slick heat of her vagina, grinding his teeth when she gripped ever so tightly around him.

"Fuck." He stiffened, grappling for control. "God . . . damn."

His control snapped like a taut power cable and he thrust greedily into her, again and again, his whole body feverish with the urgency, his body fo-cused solely on the need to mate.

The orgasm lashed out from deep in his testicles, the ejaculation so hard, he was dizzy and breathless from it. For that golden moment, he wished he could stay buried inside her for as long as his legs would let him.

He turned his head blindly, finding her mouth as she turned her face to him. The kiss was weak and calming in the aftermath of so much unleashed desire.

The warm water turned tepid against his skin, but he liked the feel of her nipple as it remained tight under his palm. She had such a soft and vulnerable look on her face, that he almost regretted not taking the time to think of something more romantic.

He kissed her again, slower, feeling oddly pro-tective.

What had he been trying to prove? That he could also enjoy sex for the sake of sex? God, couldn't she feel that she belonged in his arms? The need to do things differently bubbled up in him, but she spoke first.

"Your shirt is ruined."

"For a worthy sacrifice."

She ran her hand lazily over his shoulders, smiling. "You can't move, can you?"

"I'm surprised I can even talk right now," he admitted.

"Good."

He didn't know what to make of that, but he turned the water off and held her for a little while longer. It seemed like every surface captured their embrace. He could see their bodies mirrored on the opposite steel wall, reflected on the droplets dangling from the shower head, in the puddle of water at their feet. He wondered if she'd been watching their reflections all along.

"We should go," she finally said, with what seemed like a real shiver coursing down her spine.

He remained muddleheaded and tongue-tied as they toweled off with the clean towels in the locker, dressed and went back to the car. He popped his trunk and put on his gym shirt, handing her his towel for her hair.

On the way out, the guard raised an eyebrow, but was smart enough not to comment on his change of clothes.

chapter 7

Instead of going to the restaurant, Tanika agreed to go to his apartment for dinner, feeling both apprehensive and curious to see how he lived.

His modest condo was a classic mix of modern sculptures with some traditional pieces of furniture. Nothing impressed her more than a wall full of black-and-white photographs of people who were obviously his family. Some were in studio poses but most were informal, like the series of six where his grandmother was laughing while pushing an unruly scarf from her face. Yet another wall was dedicated to landscapes and architectural shots. She paused next to one of an old abandoned house; picture after picture had been taken of it in different seasons.

"These are lovely pictures."

"Thank you. It's the earliest family home we had."

Something in the way he said it made her look around. Sure enough, there in the entryway, in the umbrella rack, was a tripod.

"You took these pictures?" she asked.

In her modeling days, the photographers she'd worked with had all been intensely passionate about their art, taking picture after picture until they captured their vision. Well, he certainly had the intensity down, but she never would've guessed it was for photography. "These are really good. Did you study photography?"

"It's a hobby." He shrugged modestly. "What can I get you to drink?"

He was already moving into the kitchen.

She almost sputtered and instead pointed to a collage of tiny flowers. "I wish I could take artistic photos like these. I mean, these flowers are practically cheering. Mine always end up as regular snapshots."

His smile showed some pride, but he didn't respond, preferring to rummage through his cupboards for two mugs starting a kettle of water on the stove.

Tanika knew the smart thing was to drop the subject, but she now looked at every picture with new eyes, amazed at what Damon must've seen to draw him to take the photo.

She understood a bit more about him; he was the kind of man who had returned time and again to take a picture of a house that brought him fond memories, even if it was in ruins.

"How long have you been doing this?" her curiosity drove her to ask.

"Off and on since high school." He handed her a

mug of hot tea, and for the first time, she thought he looked uncomfortable with the subject. "Come on, I'll show you the rest of the house."

Okay, he definitely wanted to change the subject, so she let him. For now.

Tanika found one of his pictures in every room, some that she almost missed because they were tiny, sitting in small silver frames.

They were walking past a den when she spotted a top-of-the-line modular entertainment station, easily the envy of any serious video game player. It looked like a futuristic recliner couch with panels and controls mounted on it.

"Oh, wicked," she whispered, looking around in awe and spotting one of her favorite games. "Is that the Tribal series?"

"Did I say you could go in there?" His teasing tone took the bite out of the words.

She did a double take, then looked back into the room, which was more suited to a hard-core gamer than a corporate executive. Just how many facets were there to him?

"You any good?" he challenged.

"Any good? You are looking at the master."

His chuckle was full of wickedness.

"You're not afraid of a little competition, are you? How about we put that to the test?" she countered.

He grinned, gave her a once-over, and nodded. "Deal. But only after you get dried up and fed. Don't want you saying your fingers were too numb from being cold."

"It won't take me long to show you how it's done . . . but okay."

"I love it when you talk trash. In fact, *when* you lose, you can call me 'sir' for the rest of the night, just to spice things up a bit."

She placed a hand on her hip and bit her cheek to keep from laughing. "You must mean *if* I lose."

"Not likely. In the meantime . . . here you go." Damon handed her a couple of towels, a robe, and some clothes, then pushed her toward a bathroom to give her some privacy. "Get warmed up, eat something, then we'll battle."

Even as she showered and changed into the fresh clothes, Tanika wondered if Damon was trying to shift the relationship to a more intimate level. She tried to convince herself that his playful side was more along the lines of how Damon conducted his affairs. Surely he still understood that inviting her to his home didn't mean anything more than the inconvenience of dirtied clothes and a new location for sex.

With sex in mind, she ignored the oversized sweatshirt he'd given her in favor of his thick blue robe that almost reached her toes. Warm and naked underneath, she went in search of him and found him in the kitchen, barefoot, wearing blue plaid pajama bottoms and a white tank top. Looking like a college kid who was roaming around his dorm.

The sight of him, so at ease and masculine, inexplicably tugged at her. The appeal was more than sexual, and against her will, it seemed to lodge and glow somewhere in her chest.

As she came in, he looked up and began working a cork off a bottle of white wine.

"I could order in the Thai food, or we could make something here," he said. "I was thinking something along the lines of a salad and one of my penne specials."

"Sounds good." She shrugged, as if it didn't bother her one bit. As if the intimacy of staying at his cozy home and all it implied didn't send knots tightening in her gut.

"Want me to help with the dinner?" she asked.

"Can you put together a salad?"

"I'm no chef, but I can chop even slices of anything."

"Good enough. I'll start on the pasta."

They worked in relative silence, except for the soft music drifting from his top-of-the-line speakers. And yet there was an underlying tension that spiked every time he gave her a side glance, every time he moved behind her, like the burn from a shadow of heat.

He placed a cutting board before her, gave her a knife, and pulled out assorted vegetables from the refrigerator.

She was carefully cutting the lettuce when he brushed behind her, nibbling the curve of her shoulder. Even as a delicious shiver chased down her spine, she turned her head to look into his eyes, finding his brown, unreadable gaze darkening with sensual heat. The knife stilled in her hands.

He placed half a dozen butterfly kisses on her neck, and she arched her neck to give him more access, before his warm-breathed whisper blew into her ear. "You have sexy lips."

She licked them self-consciously. "If you want me to make the salad—"

"I'm not stopping you." His smile appeared just before he dipped his head to kiss her shoulder again. With his arms around her and his blossoming arousal against her back, she felt engulfed by him, infinitely sensual and treasured.

"Chop chop," he said, nibbling her earlobe.

"Shouldn't you be . . . ah, cooking pasta . . . or something?" Her words came out breathy, almost incoherent.

"Water's not ready." He moved to her other shoulder as she attempted to cut the lettuce again.

"I thought you could cut even slices." His chuckle rumbled against her spine.

"Bite me."

"Okay."

It was a slow bite, just on the side of her neck, the tight clench of his teeth on her skin just enough to make her gasp. At the sound, he licked the spot, nuzzling and caressing it with more kisses.

Tanika dropped the knife on the cutting board and whirled around in his arms, pulling his head to hers.

The kiss was hard and hungry, but other than rocking against her, Damon seemed to be taking his time. His hands moved up from her hips almost leisurely, cupping her breasts and caressing her nipples with his thumbs.

He kissed her until her lips were puffy and her body aching for sex. He kneaded her ass, pulled her against him, devouring her mouth until she was senseless. And still he was in no rush for more.

"I'm goddamned melting," she gasped, "and you're . . ." She made a sound of sheer frustration.

"I'm hard as a fucking steel pipe," he growled.

"I want a quickie."

"No, no, no." He brushed his lips against hers, just a breath and a touch. "I want to watch you eat when you're all horny. It's stimulating."

By the gleam in his eyes, she could see he was serious. "You're twisted."

"Yup. Then I'm going to battle you on that video game and win."

"Dream on."

"And finally, I'm going to finish what I started, which means you'll need every bit of energy from this dinner. So until then, let's get cooking."

She tugged him by his ears, frustrated yet enticed by his plans for the night. "In that case, I should warn you that the vegetables are starting to look sexy to me."

His grin flashed. "Pervert. I saw you eyeing the cucumber."

Tanika had to keep from sucking on his lips. "Five helpings of vegetables a day and all that . . ."

"And you say I'm twisted. Speaking of which . . ." He reached into his pockets and produced two star-shaped candy nipple rings.

"Naughty Devil Nipple Cherries," he said, before tearing the wrapper off the first one and holding the red candy in his hand. Tanika could only stare as he parted her robe and reached for her right breast.

"That's just . . ." She meant to say "mean," but he twisted the tiny candy star onto her already tight nipple, so it was surrounded by the candy. The jolt of it tugged at her already wet crotch, causing a tingle that all but dripped down her thighs.

"For dessert, I'm going to lick those until the candy's gone," he promised.

He slid an identical one on her left nipple, almost making her knees buckle with sheer pleasure when he lowered his head to suck her tender nipples through the tiny holes.

"I'm going to make you pay for that," she managed.

"Maybe I'll let you." He kissed her hard, then stepped back, his erection straining against the front of his pants.

"Leave the robe open," he instructed.

She could see herself naked against the reflection of the stainless steel refrigerator behind him. There she was, the terry-cloth robe open to show off the bright red star nipples against her skin. Her thighs were closed together, more to contain the wetness that surged there than anything else, but the race-stripe trim of her pubis was clearly visible.

He studied her for an endless moment, his hand moving over his covered erection in two gentle strokes, as if he were petting a savage beast into compliance.

On the stove, the pot of water suddenly bubbled louder, sending some water hissing as it boiled over.

Damon moved quickly, setting the pot on a back burner. He glanced at her, a lopsided grin appearing on his lips. "You distracted me."

She turned back to the lettuce, prepared to butcher it. "You'd better hope it doesn't take you more than ten minutes to make the dinner," she vowed. "I won't wait much longer."

"Then ten minutes it is."

The wine was perfect, the salad was a little overly diced, the pasta was just a tad undercooked, and the tomato sauce not quite warm enough, but none of it mattered.

The dinner was devoured in less time than it took them to make it.

By the time he rolled her onto the bed, her arousal was all but drooling down her thighs.

"Spermicide," she blurted, as he shucked her robe off and rolled over her to suck on a candy-covered nipple.

"What?"

She moaned and arched. "Mmm?"

"You said 'spermicide.'" He licked the candy, nipping her flesh in the center.

"Oh . . . um . . ."

He lifted his head and waited, his heavy breaths fanning over her skin.

"No condom," she clarified, swallowing past the dryness in her throat. "I want to feel you. So I used some spermicide."

If possible, his eyes blazed more strongly. "How long does it take to activate?"

"Ten minutes."

His smile gleamed. "Ah-ha. What a coincidence."

She tugged him back over her and kissed him hard. Enough was enough! She wanted—needed—to have him or she was simply going to explode.

Between grappling caresses and demanding kisses, his clothes came off. Her nipples were swollen and tight to the point of pain, but still he licked and sucked the candy, bringing the taste of cherry to her mouth when he finally chewed the last of the cherry from her.

By the time his fingers stroked her clitoris, she was whimpering and wriggling, her hand searching for and finding his engorged erection to slide into her.

He yanked her hands away, his breathing ragged. She growled and shoved hard enough to roll him onto his back, then nimbly shifted over his cock and slid slick and wet, onto him, flesh on flesh, the incredible sensation of his skin and muscle kneading and plunging into her, spearing past her nether lips in hot fusion.

His moan and her broken cry mingled in the passing seconds as the sensation of him filled her.

"God . . . God, Damon . . ."

She moved first, riding him hard, mouth open and gasping, eyes closed in the mindless growing ecstasy. He thrust upward to match her downward rhythm, then stroked her clit when she started to clench above him.

"Come on, babe," he whispered, "Gimme . . ."

She screamed in silence and sank her fingernails into his shoulders when he half sat up, clenched his arm around her waist and clamped her in place, impaling his thrust.

The waves of the orgasm hit her like tiny sonic booms that clenched him deep in her vagina. She felt the delightful and sudden liquid heat of his ejaculation, then rocked into him, brainlessly taking more.

She clung to him, her abraded breasts against his, her perspiring belly on his, her trembling hips locked with his, rocking together . . . slower and slower.

He tumbled her over and thrust into her some more, shuddering with every plunge until there was nothing more she could take.

He collapsed over her, crowding her, breathing in her hot breaths until he mustered enough energy to flop onto his back and pull her limp form to his side.

Seconds later, she was fast asleep.

When she was awakened later, it was to the scent of verdant tea and ginger, the oils of which were being rubbed over her skin by firm, skilled hands.

They touched in the dark, barely talking, covering each other with the sensitizing ND oils he'd pulled out from somewhere. Slippery and perfumed, they made love again, her thighs so oiled, she struggled to grip his hips.

The third orgasm was the strongest, sucking her in and imploding in her until she felt like little more than floating white smoke.

It was pitch-dark when she became aware of Damon's steady heartbeat beneath her ear and of his flaccid penis still pressing against her.

Her lips tingled when she pressed them together. For that matter, her vaginal folds also tingled, and she remembered the nerve-sensitizing orgasm.

Carefully, she stretched away from him, hearing his soft moan when their bodies separated. Then as he began to breathe softly, she covered him with a blanket and silently tiptoed into the bathroom.

Dazed, she sat on the edge of the tub, her skin

feeling ultrasensitive against the terry-cloth robe, the depths of her overly tender sex tingling as if Damon were still mounted inside her.

God, he'd done it again and probably had no idea he was having such an effect on her. He'd been fun, but she'd had lovers that were fun before. He'd been good in bed, and admittedly, better than any lover before. But there was more.

If she wasn't careful, she was going to fall for him . . .

Part of her wanted to rush back to the bed, to snuggle up to him and push all the heavy thinking away until dawn. The other part of her warned that this was where she had to make her point and leave.

Stay-overs and romantic dinners were what traditional lovers did when they intended to get serious and move the relationship into deeper waters.

Man, wasn't it bad enough she'd opted for the spermicide rather than the condom?

She had to get out before he got the wrong idea and this became a whole new type of relationship. He'd warned her he only wanted a couple of days of sex. He had even compared it to a good game of racquetball.

Yes, staying would just send him mixed messages.

The relationship had exceeded its three-day limit, right? Why push her luck?

Once again, she sat in the dark way too long, debating how to end the evening.

Finally, she cleaned up, donned her clothes, and called a taxi to take her home, trying like hell to ignore the little voice that warned her she was making a big mistake.

chapter 8

Damon glanced around his pristine office, remembering how he had awakened in the dark of the night, reached for Tanika, and discovered that she wasn't there. The dregs of sleep had made the bulky shadows of the room give him the illusion that she was next to him, and tricked him into calling out her name only to hear the question fall silently in the room.

The need to hold her had been so basic and elemental, he'd buried his face in her pillow just to have something to hold.

Hell, he'd woken up smelling like a flower shop and gleaming like his grandmother's mahogany dinner table. Friggin' ND oils!

Goddammit.

There was no excuse for why it felt like claws were sinking into his heart every time he thought of her closing the door as she left. Hadn't he told her once before not to leave without letting him know? Was she so determined to draw the line that she couldn't even extend him that simple courtesy?

He couldn't shake it off. He was getting involved, and as much as he didn't want to, he couldn't change the way he felt now.

If they were to have any kind of a relationship, there had to be some personal respect. He wanted to be able to take her to a restaurant every now and then and not just plow her into a wall for a quick fuck.

He took a deep breath, then let it out slowly before reaching for his mug of coffee.

He wasn't going to let her get away that easily.

She could play the disinterested card all she wanted, but he knew that come nighttime, she'd be looking to scratch that sex itch again.

He could play, too. And this time, he'd be ready.

Outside his office, people were already heading to the scheduled morning meeting, but he held back, gathering last-minute reports from his computer, and keeping an eye out for Tanika.

He was tired of thinking of her, of wanting her when he didn't want to want her. At least not to this degree.

Nonetheless, he couldn't get her out of his mind.

The printer blinked a red light at him and he jabbed at several display buttons.

"Your technical skills are a little lacking this morning," his grandmother said reproachfully as she entered his office. It was nerve-racking when she did her soundless vampire appearances like that.

He resisted the urge to give the computer a solid thump on its side. "We need faster printers."

"Glaring at it won't make it work any faster."

"For the price we paid for them—" He bit back a filthy profanity when the printer made a harsh grinding noise, jamming with half a page sticking out.

"Not your morning, I see."

He started poking and checking the usual faulty components of the printer.

"Aren't you late for your meeting?"

He gritted his teeth. From the corner of his eye, he saw her step further into the room, and when he glanced at her, she was sniffing the air. "I smell green tea," she said with a startled look on her face. "And white ginger . . . Well, well."

Mentally, he cringed, knowing the last comment was anything but good.

"I guess I'll have to make do without this particular report," he said, giving up on the printer.

"You know who also smelled like white ginger and tea this morning?"

Oh, Lordy.

"Speaking of tea, you'd smell it if you were drinking it," he replied, noticing that the liquid in her mug looked suspiciously like coffee. "Didn't your doctor tell you to stay away from coffee?"

"I've been drinking coffee since I was six. Don't try to lecture me on my health, Damon." Her lips pursed and her eyebrow arched. "And where were you last night? I called a couple of times, but got your voice mail."

He simultaneously reached for the small phone

on his belt clip, but stopped, suddenly noticing the weariness of her face. "Why? What happened?"

"Nothing happened but dinner. I was making your favorite shrimp marsala and—"

"You're supposed to stay away from shellfish, too."

She sighed, muttering with refined annoyance. "Damon, I'd rather die with a bellyful of marsala than live the next twenty years eating nothing but alfalfa sprouts. And yes, I brought you the leftovers."

"You are a saint."

"And don't you forget it. Speaking of which, I'm not planning on going to Lake Tahoe this New Year. I forgot to give them notice, so the room is yours if you want it."

He stared blankly at her, his gut feeling like it was bottoming out. She'd been going to Tahoe for as long as he could remember. "Why aren't you going?"

"My bones can't handle the cold anymore." She shrugged a delicate shoulder. "Don't make a big deal of it, Damon. I'd just rather be here in the warmth of my own home."

"The hotel rooms are suitably heated."

"As is my house."

"Then what is it?"

"It's nothing. You'll miss their fireworks. You should go."

"What are your plans?"

"San Francisco puts on a great show. I think I'll hang around to see them for a change."

When he didn't respond, she smiled softly at him. "Don't be a worrywart. Go to Tahoe for me, okay? I insist."

"No way—"

"Did you make plans for New Year's?"

"No, but—"

"Then go! Enjoy it! It will make me happy to think of you there."

The helpless churning in his gut got worse.

"Damon, really," she huffed, then turning on her heel, she looked over her shoulder before she left. "Please try to make it to the meeting in the next few minutes. I deplore tardiness."

He tugged his ear in frustration. Women!

What on earth was he going to do about them? He exhaled and made a mental note to contact her doctor. Not that the man would divulge anything, but it might be worth a try.

He turned back to his desk, grabbed his reports, and headed out the door.

It had proven to be a long day, starting when Tanika had entered the meeting late, hoping she looked smart and chipper instead of feeling like a woman who had crept out on her lover.

In fact, he looked at her as indifferently as if they might have had lunch together once. It was a strain to play along.

The meeting had droned on, but she'd found herself admiring his movements when he'd removed his jacket and rolled his shirtsleeves up to get down to business. He'd played it cool while having to look over the latest batch of catalog thongs and bras selected for the February sales event.

When the meeting was over, he'd stayed to take a phone call, and Tanika had reluctantly left.

Back at her desk, she engrossed herself in work, eating a sandwich over her keyboard for lunch, then catching up on calls and e-mails in the afternoon.

By the end of the day, the need to see him was like hungering for a chocolate fix. She simply had to have it.

On impulse, she picked up her phone and dialed his number.

"Becker," he replied, over the busy keyboard tapping in the background.

She put on her sexiest voice. "Sleek boats . . . rudders . . . original wood paneling . . ."

The typing stopped and she imagined him reclining in his chair. "I love it when you talk dirty."

"I'd go on, but that's about the extent of it," she admitted.

"What? No talk about anchors?"

"Hmm . . . How about we discuss it over dinner?"

He sighed. "Can't. I've already made plans for the evening."

That caught her off guard. "Oh."

"With my grandmother."

She hadn't realized how tense she was until his answer came. "Okay."

"Rain check?"

"Sure." Then because she wasn't quite ready to hang up, she recrossed her legs and blurted, "How about New Year's? It's the day after tomorrow."

There was the tiniest pause. "Sure. As a matter of fact, I've just been offered a place in Lake Tahoe where there are great fireworks."

Wow. "That sounds great."

"How about I pick you up tomorrow?"

"Perfect."

They said their goodbyes and she hung up, wondering what the next few days would bring. It was getting close to when one of them had to make the decision to break it off.

As much as she enjoyed Damon, she had to make the break first. The timing would be excellent. They could wrap up the old year—as well as their fling— then start the new year without ties.

Damon moved his ivory chess piece, and waited for his grandmother to make her next move.

While he waited, he poured more of her favorite peach tea into one of her finest porcelain teacups. The set had been a gift her husband had given her once, when they'd first been married, and although two of the teacups were chipped and three of the saucers showed nicks, Damon noticed that she always beamed when she used them.

It was also the reason they were playing chess

instead of slamming down some dominoes. The dominoes had been his grandfather's and there were some things that still hurt her too much.

He settled back into his chair, wishing he'd thought to bring his beloved camera.

"You've got that shutterbug gleam in your eye again. What kind of pictures are you taking these days?"

"Oh, nothing much. I took some great shots of the boats heading out of the bay. And of course, the Golden Gate Bridge is still one of my favorite subjects."

She chuckled as she looked over the chessboard. "I remember when you used to take pictures of it with the cheap disposable cameras."

He smiled fondly, remembering how many lawns he'd had to cut to pay for getting his favorite photos printed on quality paper. "Not the best, but I learned a lot from those cheapies."

Her wrinkled hands reached for her black knight and he instantly guessed her next move before she made it.

She sighed. "What's on your mind, honey?"

"Nothing. Can't I just come by, pay you a visit, and challenge you to a game of chess?"

She glanced at the bouquet of flowers he'd brought her and blew gently on her tea without comment.

Here in her parlor, there was never any talk of work, so he suspected the tea party would last a while.

"Leaving the old year always used to make your father melancholy," she said. "Seems to me you have the end-of-the-year blues, too."

She looked up at him inquiringly, but he couldn't tell her how he felt. How could he explain that he had come because he was worried about her? No, she wouldn't want to talk about that. Maybe he could explain that he didn't trust himself to succumb to sex with Tanika. Lord knew he was on the brink of behaving like a depraved addict, or worse, setting himself up to fall in love.

Her wrinkled hands cupped the fragile teacup, holding it like a nest in her hands. Already he could imagine a black-and-white photo of the image, except he'd keep that rich tannic color of the tea to make it stand out.

"You could be with her right now."

His grandmother's words jolted him from his thoughts. "Who?"

She rolled her eyes. "You know who. The one who's making you stare at my tea and fall into daydreams."

He grabbed one of her neatly stacked cookies and popped it whole into his mouth, shrugging when she raised an eyebrow, waiting for a response.

When she didn't get one, she said, "Did I ever tell you about the time I was nineteen and dated this guy named Dan? He was charming, and a gentleman. Every time he came calling, he'd bring me flowers. I thought for sure he was the one, but then I took my

car to get my brakes fixed, and Jamus slid out from
under a car, his face streaked with oil, his overalls
dirty, and a rag sticking out his back pocket." She
smiled and took a sip. "I fell in love just like that. It
was like he'd snatched my heart right out of my
chest. I knew I was a goner."

She touched the rim of her teacup, then seemed
to remember the game and moved her ivory bishop.
"In fact, I kept going back to his shop, complaining
about strange noises that just weren't there. And all
the flowers in the world wouldn't have changed the
way I felt."

"Love will do that to you," he replied.

"Yep. It comes out of nowhere and sure makes
you do some strange things."

Like stare into tea cups? His gut clenched and he
eyed the game board, wondering if she realized she'd
left her queen vulnerable in order to carry on the conversation.

"Are you ever going to get around to telling me
what your doctor said?"

"I'm sure he'd say I'm doing just fine for a
woman my age."

Humph. "And yet you won't go to Lake Tahoe?"

"That's right. I won't. Something tells me you'd
make better use of the place."

He ignored her vulnerable queen and went for her
bishop. "How about a trade-off? I'll confirm that rumor if you tell me what the doctor said."

"Of course it's not rumor, Damon, just my clever

intuition. You've been coming in late and smelling like ginger. What's a person to assume?"

"You have been drinking coffee even though your visits to your doctor have become more frequent. What's a person to assume?"

She tromped his knight with her queen. "One can assume I like coffee."

"Yeah, and one can assume I enjoy walking around smelling like ginger, too."

She smiled and wiggled her eyebrows at him. "Do you?"

He countered by knocking her queen off the board. "Checkmate."

"Drat." She studied the board for a few seconds more. "All right. Fair enough. The old fart thinks I need new scans."

"The old fart? You mean Dr. Wagner?"

"That would be him."

"Why? It's those chest pains, isn't it?"

She slid back, relaxing slightly toward one armrest, and took another sip of tea. "I had a minor episode," she said on a sigh.

No . . . "Not minor enough if he's taking scans."

She frowned. "I've said enough. Your turn."

Damn stubborn woman! He gathered up the pieces of the abandoned game and began to put them away. "I've been seeing someone."

"Who also happens to enjoy ginger?"

"Maybe."

"Who is she?"

"I don't kiss and tell, Grandma, you know that."

"I also know it's someone at work."

There was no way she was going to make him confirm that. "So, has Wagner put you on any new medication?"

"Are you serious about this one or am I going to die before I ever see my great-grandkids?"

"Jesus Christ!" Frozen, he stared at her. Die?

"Relax. I didn't imply you should impregnate the first woman you see . . ."

"Thank God!"

". . . but it would be nice to have an adorable infant to bounce on my knee. Before I'm dead would be nice." She grinned.

"Would you stop with that word!"

She calmly sipped her tea, an indulgent look on her face. "Boy, even I cannot live forever. Now, come on, tell me about your girl."

He refilled her teacup. Die? She was tossing that word around like it was nothing and he was supposed to be calm about it?

"Ahem . . ."

"I'm not in love, Grandma. And I wish you'd tell me what's really going on with your health."

"I'm old. My body has issues. It happens." She waved a hand as if dispersing smoke. "Tell me more about Ms. Ginger Tea."

He ran a hand over his face. "Sounds to me like we're at a stalemate."

"All right, all right. How about just a hint?"

"Nope. But I'll tell you what. If you let me see your heart scans when they come in, I'll tell you what you want to know."

She smiled, her eyes twinkling over the teacup. "You have yourself a deal."

Rather than risk having Damon come to her apartment, Tanika stayed up the night before and packed for the trip to Lake Tahoe. In the morning, she'd crammed the bags into the trunk of her car, wondering what Damon would make of her preparedness.

At work, the day went on endlessly, with Tanika thinking and analyzing the risks of spending New Year's with Damon.

As the last of the employees left the building, she touched up her makeup in the restroom mirror, hoping all signs of her restless night were erased.

After a quick fluff of her hair, she left the building and headed for the almost empty parking lot. Once again, their cars were side by side.

Damon stood by his SUV, making her ache to rush over and kiss him. More and more, the gleam in his eyes made her feel like he was reading her thoughts, so she kept her stroll casual. If anyone were to see them, they were no more than two coworkers gabbing in the parking lot.

"Ready to go?" he asked.

"Yes. Sure am."

"Want me to follow you to your place for the luggage—"

"I packed it in my car already."

There was just a slight hesitation. "Ah." She pressed a button on her key chain and her trunk popped open.

Ever the gentleman, Damon opened the passenger door so she could step into his car while he moved her luggage over to his vehicle.

Moments later, he was in the driver's seat and they were on the highway toward Lake Tahoe. She'd expected him to make some comment about her being packed and ready, but he remained quiet.

The awkward tension between them persisted as he asked if she wanted her seat adjusted, the air vent tilted, or even a bottle of water for the long trip. To her ears, her replies sounded stiff, and it was all she could do not to squirm in her seat.

"Tip back your seat and relax. We'll be there shortly," he said, sounding like a pilot readying for takeoff.

Ding! Fasten your seat belts!

This is a nonsmoking flight.

For your safety, do not lean over and fondle the pilot's formidable and suckable package while he's going ninety on the freeway . . .

"What's got you smiling?"

"Um, nothing. Just . . ." Exploring a fantasy.

"Just looking forward to the weekend." She ruined it by not being able to hold back a yawn.

"Tired?"

"Just a little. You?"

"I'm good."

Yes. Yes, he certainly was. She looked out her window at the scenery rushing by, wondering if she should just blurt out what was on her mind. Or not.

Perhaps it was the long day, or the calm that overcame her just to be with him, but she fell asleep as they were heading up the foothills.

She slept so soundly, that it was only when he shook her that she realized they had reached their destination and a valet was approaching the vehicle to open her door.

Straightening her hair and trying to look awake, Tanika stepped out into a world of bright lights, cool wind, and the jackpot noises clanging from gambling machines.

There were swarms of people everywhere and it was a relief when they were finally standing in a spacious and opulent master suite, their luggage not far behind. The view was even more stunning.

"How did you manage this suite on such short notice?" she asked.

"I know someone who knows someone."

"Nice pull."

He eyed her as he removed his jacket. Dressed in his black turtleneck and black jeans, he was easy to gawk at. He was the perfect blend of gentleman and businessman. "You've been quiet. What's on your mind?"

She settled on the edge of the bed as he approached her. "We both know it's been leading up to this," she began, studying her shoes. "But, well . . ."

He tipped her chin upward with his hand. "Just tell me."

Hell, it had to be done. "I'd like this weekend to be the end of it."

His touch felt warm on her chin. "Of us," he corrected.

"Yes."

He paused, his hand dropping away. "I was thinking the same thing."

Really? How long had he been thinking that?

"Out with the old habits, in with the new, right?" he added casually.

"Right." So, she was an old habit?

He checked his watch. "It's almost nine, do you want to grab a bite at a restaurant or should I have something sent up?"

Tanika felt as if she'd lost her bearings slightly. "What's your preference?"

He pushed her backward into the mattress. "Eating in. This way, I get to talk you into letting me take pictures of you."

"Pictures? No way." His cologne, she realized, was still that classic familiar scent she'd always think of as his alone. Timeless.

"You won't have to be naked."

"Well, that makes it better," she teased. "What if I want to take pictures of you?"

"From the waist up? Sure."

She chuckled. "You've thought this one through."

He brushed her lips with a kiss. "It will be the next-to-last thing I ever ask of you," he promised.

"Really? What would be the very last thing?"

He gave her earlobe a soft bite before answering. "Uh-uh. All in good time."

Then he pushed off the bed and went for the phone, ordering from room service. Photos? Maybe she should've expected it, but the truth was, she hadn't. His pictures at home had been so tasteful, she knew he'd never ask anything crude of her. But still, was he intending a final wrap-up, such as "Sayonara, sister, and by the way, here are some photos"?

Man, she was thinking too hard.

Tanika began going through her packed clothes for her negligees, while he ordered a variety of appetizers along with side salads.

He paused in the middle of his conversation on the phone to point and say, "The bronze one," before getting back on the line and adding wine to the order.

No. She had no problem wearing a negligee to a photo shoot when it was for work, because the truth was, it was easy to think of herself as a model.

But tonight, Damon wasn't planning on capturing

the lingerie at its best. He wasn't asking her to strike a pose to sell a product.

He was asking to capture *her*.

And it frightened her a bit to know that he had the skill to do it, to steal her soul through the magic of his lens.

Steal? No, he couldn't steal something she wasn't willing to give up. If anything, she'd make damned sure he only saw what she wanted to portray, and that was that!

When she came out of the bathroom, he had his sleeves rolled up, and a bulky camera in his hands. "Ready?"

She shrugged.

"Tanika, by now you must know me well enough to realize that I won't take photos you don't want me to. I'm not taking nudie shots or anything like that."

"Of course, because I will absolutely not allow nude shots. But incidentally, if I have to be in one little bittie item of clothing, then you do, too."

He grinned and started by kicking off his shoes. "No problem."

"I want your word no one but us will see these photos, Damon."

"You have my word."

The tension between her shoulders eased; she knew she could count on him. "How long is the shoot?"

"I don't know if 'shoot' is the right word. It'll just be a casual thing. No biggie."

"Sure, you say that now, but I'm the one who's half naked."

"All right. I'll even the odds." He stripped down to his boxers, then held his hand out.

"What?"

"Come here."

She stood and he pulled her forward so she was crushed gently to his chest. His warm skin had her body immediately reacting. "You're too tensed up," he observed.

"Am not."

"Are, too. Plus, you're missing something." His mouth swooped down on hers, giving her the kiss she'd been craving since she'd walked up to him in the parking lot.

Endless moments later, when it ended, she was breathless and definitely aroused. "Oh, that . . . Can't believe I was missing that."

"No prob. If you forget again, I'll point it out."

"Hmmm." She smiled, feeling like a dreamy-eyed teenager.

"And listen, if you're uncomfortable posing for me, I understand. I'm not trying to get sex-kitten shots. I just want pictures of you."

Yes, it was exactly what she was afraid of. Pictures that would reveal too much of her, beyond skin and clothes.

"Are you cool with that?" he asked.

"Yes. I'm cool."

He touched his right thumb over her lips as if to

keep himself from kissing her again. "Go ahead and sit down and I'll set up some lights."

She'd slipped on her silk robe because she'd started to get cold, then sat on the plush queen's chair with her feet tucked beneath her.

She watched the muscles flex as he set up his tripod, then attached his camera.

The silence between them hummed with anticipation.

"Relax." He pressed a couple of buttons on his camera, held a little device near the light, and to her surprise, ended up next to her with a remote control in his hand.

"Ready?"

Tanika laced her fingers and smiled. "Cheese."

He chuckled, deep in his chest.

She gestured aimlessly. "I guess I'm not sure what you want me to do."

That gave him pause. "Close your eyes and think of something pleasant . . . like those Naughty Devil edible boxer shorts."

"Cute." She closed her eyes, even though she could hear him shifting closer. The kiss landed on her lips just as she was trying to conjure up the product.

It was a midnight kiss, subtly different from the last. It was the kind of kiss that was slow and tingly, all moonlight and romance. The kind that came after carnival rides and shoulder massages. The kind with just enough heat to rekindle sex in the middle of the night.

It only lasted a second, but her heart kicked a little faster, and her breathing jogged up, as well.

"Are you mentally munching on boxers?" he asked huskily.

"Nibbling actually."

He stole another kiss. "My kind of woman. No, no. Keep your eyes closed."

He stepped away from her then, and she heard the distinct camera click.

"Hey, no fair."

"I just wanted to capture that hungry, sexy look you have on your face."

Damn . . .

She peeked and watched him move behind the camera, the bulge of his erection pushing against the front of his boxer shorts like a fist. "You are so hot when you are hungry for more."

The camera clicked again. She didn't know what to say, but sex seemed like a safe enough topic.

"So . . . do you want me to talk dirty now?" she taunted.

Click.

"If you like. No boats or anchors, though." He peeked around the camera, his skin like a shadow. She closed her eyes again.

"Um, okay, then where do I start?"

He paused. "I'd love to know what it feels like to you, when I'm inside you."

Oh! Christ . . .

Click.

She licked her lips. Okay, she could do this. "It's . . . unique."

The camera made a quiet whirling sound. Was he zooming in?

His voice rumbled toward her, a soft murmur. "Sex with you is unique for me, too."

"I like the feel of your skin in me . . . and on me. I don't think I've ever gotten really sweaty before, but . . . I just—we just end up that way."

She could hear the change in his breathing as the camera clicked.

"Look at me."

She did, barely making him out behind the camera.

"You feel like honeyed velvet when I'm inside you."

Her nipples tightened painfully and the camera clicked again.

His voice all but hypnotized her. "I couldn't get enough of those candy nipple rings. I'd love to play with those on you again."

Tanika licked her lips, feeling flushed and aroused.

"I love finding all those places where you hide tasty flavors for me. All those sexy lotions and perfumes."

She pushed her thighs together, shifting just slightly, then caught herself.

Click.

"I do so love your mouth . . ."

Click.

"And your hands . . ."

Click.

"And the way you make those soft, yearning sounds just before you come . . ."

She pushed away from the chair before she'd realized it. "Stop."

He stood as well, several feet separating them. "Do you really want me to?"

She didn't know where to start. Couldn't even put into words how she felt. He was so effortlessly breaking down her barriers until she felt completely naked.

"You are the most alluring woman I know . . . I find myself wanting to taste you . . . to sample that unique taste you leave on my fingertips . . . or that curved dip in your spine . . . or that dip at the base of your neck. I could lick and lick and never forget the taste."

The hot intensity in his eyes captured hers. She stood there, speechless.

In half a second, he'd unhooked the camera from the tripod and snapped her picture again.

It's just about sex, she told herself. This was only about sex, so why not indulge him? But her sexy smart-alecky remarks escaped her, leaving her with nothing to say.

"But then you get this look in your eye." His husky murmurs continued, his camera clicking like an extension of his words.

"And that's all it takes for the essence of you to come back to me. All of you."

Emotion formed like a stone in her throat even as desire welled inside her. Goddamn him! Her heart felt trapped and swollen, trembling like a caged bird.

She wanted him, needed him, she realized, not just for an hour, a day, or even a weekend. She wanted him for a very long, long time. Maybe forever . . .

Click.

He lowered the camera and looked at her, his chest gently billowing with each breath he took.

It hit her like one of his kisses, soft and seductive and dumbfounding.

She was falling in love with him.

God, no . . .

"Am I the only one feeling this way?" he asked quietly, lowering the camera. A shadow of hurt came and went over his face and she realized she'd taken too long to speak.

"No! No, that's not it. Sorry." She sat back down on shaky legs. "It's just that . . . I thought that . . . You, you know . . . you—"

"I've got too many skills to just pick one, huh?" he teased, forcing a smile.

Their eyes held for a long hungry pause. "Yes." God's truth . . .

But *love*?

When had it happened? She couldn't *love* him!

Not after agreeing with him that they'd go their separate ways the following day. This was just a fling, anyway. A harmless, fun, sporty fling. How could this be LOVE?

Shit.

She closed her eyes, trying to hide the realization that her world had irrevocably started spinning in the opposite direction.

Click. The sound shattered the silence and crashed into her thoughts like thunder.

Jolted by the sound, she stood again. "I—I need a breather."

He put the camera down. "Okay."

She could feel him watching her still as she went to the windows and looked out. From floor to ceiling the world of Lake Tahoe lay before her, the buildings like clusters of burning gems in the charcoal blackness of night.

The windows were thick, and from their base, a light blue neon glow seemed trapped, illuminating the room with soft light.

"Tanika?"

Damon's image moved like a ghost behind her, his reflection in the glass encroaching. The backlight was too dim to reveal more than his male shape.

"It's beautiful down there, isn't it?" she asked.

"Gorgeous."

A single shimmer of light burst in the sky.

"Fireworks?" she asked in surprise.

"Yes, but that's nothing compared to what they'll do tomorrow. They pull out all the stops."

The silence stretched along with the tension.

He moved closer, until her back was completely against his front. He wound his arms around her and for several moments, they simply looked down at the ribbons of traffic, at the bright gambling lights that contrasted sharply with such a black, still night.

He kissed her neck, and she sighed. She loved him . . .

This was what they had, what worked so well. Well, then, she'd take as much of it as she could.

Arching her neck, she murmured his name. He lightly ran his hands over her shoulders, but she pulled them to her breasts. Reaching for the edge of her robe, she tugged it over her shoulders.

He followed the arch of her neck down to one of her bare collarbones.

The bite he left there sent a melting shiver down her spine, but when he tried to turn her around, she held still.

"Tanika—"

"Shh . . ."

She took her right hand and slowly, carefully, placed it on the window glass. She could see the silhouette of their faces there and the way their hands looked so good side by side.

He took her other hand and placed it on the opposite side, moving closer still and nudging her feet apart.

Her heart thundered and she waited, so eager, so impatient, so full of this brimming emotion.

He nuzzled her ear, nipping while his hands roamed over her breasts. She wondered if anyone would think to look up at their room, or even if anything could be seen from the outside.

Still nuzzling her ear, Damon cupped her breasts and caressed them, massaging them. His hands felt familiar as they handled the weight of each mound of flesh, teasing the tips of her breasts, and half rolling the nipple as they tugged outward. Tanika moaned, desperately wishing his mouth was there, and sure he knew it.

His breathing deepened, got rougher, but then, so did hers.

He kissed down her neck again, moving to her spine and working his way to her other ear, all the while slowly caressing her breasts until they felt swollen and achy.

Damon seemed completely engrossed in his exploration, but when she moved her right hand to touch his face, he made a "tsk-tsk" sound and returned her hand to the windowpane.

On the other end of the lake, the first burst of fireworks seared the sky, powdering it briefly in shaky streaks of blue.

His fingers moved to the sash of the robe and undid the bow, letting it drop unheeded to the floor. Three dashes of red fireworks flashed into the heavens as his hands roamed her torso . . . spanning her ribs, moving over her belly button and rubbing it, then lower, covering her sex.

"Damon . . . the bed," she whispered.

"Hush. Let me feel you."

Her legs were pushed wider, and his fingers grew bolder, moving more intimately between her thighs, finding the crest of her clit, then following down like petals to nectar. Yes, she'd used the Sugar Cane Honey, but could he smell it, too?

She gasped, enduring the sweet, knowing touch of his hand, then groaning again when his other hand slid down and joined in, holding the folds of her nether lips open with one hand to delve and stroke her deeper, his knuckles rubbing with a gentle roughness as his fingers thrust deeper.

"Oh, God . . ." She'd never been touched like that before, with both hands, so completely invasive and incredibly intimate.

Her eyes slid shut just as fireworks burst like huge yellow dandelions at a distance.

He dipped in with one hand, gathering her wetness and rolling it up to her clit so his other hand could caress the flesh there.

His erection strained at her back, made even more sensuous by her silk robe between them.

His caresses worked too well, making her dizzy, achy, and moaning with the urgent need to come. He rocked against her from behind, stroking her lubricated sex in his hands in the front while rubbing his cock against her behind.

She swallowed dryly, moaning weakly. Her legs trembled as he pushed her ever so slightly forward, and she felt the strength of his thighs behind hers.

"Please," she pleaded, opening her eyes and trying to meet his in the reflection but encountering only a dark silhouette.

A spiral of green started another firework, and for half a second, she saw his face as he kissed her gently on her neck.

Damon, oh . . . God!

Her legs almost buckled when he abruptly moved his hands up to cup her breasts again. Her clit ached, the flesh there practically humming, and the throat of her vagina throbbed with a viscous empty pulse.

His fingers kneaded her breasts with a little less restraint, the slickness of her arousal mixed with Savage Rose lotion scenting the air.

She tossed her head, her hands shifting against the glass, unable to find reprieve.

Once again, his mouth moved to her spine, and for a long hard pause, she felt his forehead rest there as he fought for control.

More fireworks speared into the sky, shattering apart without a sound to her ears, looking glorious in its destruction.

Giving in to the slightest pressure from his head, Tanika leaned forward even more, until her face was so close to the glass that her panting breaths came back to her.

His hands left her breast, and with slow tugs, the

Japanese robe was lifted, gathered over the back of her calves and thighs, until it was piled onto the small of her back.

With the barrier gone between them, she felt both overexposed and vulnerable, and yet hot and expectant. The thick heat of his cock jammed against her thigh, then shifted until it was right on the portal of her aroused nether lips, brushing against her like a coital kiss.

As he bent over her, Damon's hands went back to her vagina, working the head of his cock about half an inch in, rubbing it out, while his fingers stroked, rolled, and circled her clit.

Her legs trembled and she buckled slightly, taking another inch by sheer accident.

He groaned, the sound ending like a growl by her ear.

More explosions and light dazzled on the horizon, but she was almost oblivious of the colors as he shifted, deeper, thicker, perfecting the erotic synchronization of his hands.

He nipped her shoulder like a stallion on a mare, then rode her deeper still, the rugged momentum of the thrust jabbing, then withdrawing, again . . . repeating over and over.

Tanika begged and pleaded, her cheek touching the cool glass and shifting against the window with each rocking motion.

As his thrusts became harder, one of his hands came up to cup her left breast, his other steadily circling and stroking her perked clitoris until it was just too much and she came with a sharp cry, standing on her toes and rocking her ass backward to draw out his fullness inside her trembling, sucking womb.

It seemed to snap the last of his control, and his hands settled roughly on her hips, holding her in a firm grip as he pounded out his own release with a broken grunt.

chapter 9

Damon sensed the change in Tanika like a cool wind over his skin. She'd made love with a desperation he hadn't seen before, and he could've sworn there had been tears in her eyes when he'd carried her to bed.

The silence had become intense as they'd recovered, huddled together under the sheets, each lost in private thoughts.

He figured he'd give her a few minutes more when she abruptly sat up in bed and stalked off toward his camera. He sat up, unsure what she'd do next.

She raised it to her eye, aimed it at him like a sniper's crosshairs and clicked. "Your turn."

He leaned back against the pillows, not entirely relaxed. She smiled, but he sensed anger . . . no, anger was the wrong word, but it was something just as volatile.

"When I first met you," she said, returning to the bed, "I was sure you were too uptight to have an affair. I didn't think you were the type for a fling."

"I'm not," he admitted. "But I'm no saint, either."

She leisurely took pictures, zooming in on his arms, his chest. "Does that make you a sinner?"

"Are you feeling philosophical?"

"Just wondering."

She moved to another angle, taking pictures of his legs.

"I don't know much about saints or sinners. I just know what I like," he said.

She pointed the camera at his knees, and he wondered why she had yet to take any pictures of his face.

"You know a lot about sex." She snapped a picture of his hand holding the sheets over his groin. It was the one shot he'd expected.

"Is that a complaint?"

"No." She turned the camera to his toes. "On the contrary."

She clicked at random, his knees, his hands, his shoulders. Anything but his face.

"Hey . . ."

She peered at him over the camera and he tried to read the emotions that warred in her eyes, wondering if he'd really seen tears starting to well in her eyes. Intuitively, he reached for her. "Hey, honey, what is it?"

The camera covered her eyes and she took the first few pictures of his face.

"You've got a great dick," she murmured, still hiding behind the lens and clicking away. "I could ride you right now and take pictures of your face as you come."

He waited for her to lower the camera but she didn't. "Is that what you want?"

"Don't you?" She took two rapid shots and peeked at him just as the knock came on the door announcing room service.

Damon rolled off the bed and, on his way to the door, shrugged on his robe.

The aromatic carts of food were rolled in, and as soon as they were alone again, Damon took some spare towels, laid them on the floor by the large windows.

"What are you doing?" she asked, finally putting the camera down.

"Setting up for our picnic."

He busied himself moving the coffee table closer to the towels while she propped herself up on her elbows and watched. "Hungry?" he asked.

"Starved."

He opened his arms wide. "Well, you'd better come down here then while there's still food left."

Wrapped up in the bedsheets, she wriggled out of the bed, her hair a seductive array. The cautious look on her face gripped his heart to the point of bursting. Man, if he didn't tread carefully, she'd probably leave.

"Grab a couple of pillows, would you, darlin'?"

She seemed startled by the endearment, and didn't hide it fast enough.

"Sure, snookums," she said lightly, but he could tell that it was a knee-jerk reaction.

He sat on the towel and patted the space next to him, attempting to lighten the mood. "Get your curvy butt over here."

She threw the pillows at him. "Is curvy the polite way to say big?"

He caught the pillows midair. "Just how stupid do you think I am?"

She harrumphed, then walked over, trailing the bedsheets in her wake with the grace of a princess. She didn't protest when he pulled her close to his side and they settled into the pillows to view the last of the fireworks. Still, it took a glass of wine before she truly began to relax against him.

Half turned toward her, he fed her a slice of melon, enthralled by how the fruit disappeared between her lips.

"Do you have big plans for tomorrow?" she asked.

"Actually, yes."

"Such as?"

He chewed on melon as well. "How do you feel about horses?"

"You mean those creatures with big teeth and hefty hoofs?"

"Yup."

"I like them just fine." She raised a thin slice of apple to her mouth. "And if they go really fast, I've even been known to bet on them."

He grabbed a slice of apple as well and chewed. "Good. But we won't be betting on them or looking at the size of their teeth."

She sipped wine. "We won't?"

"No. The room comes with a ride down one of the scenic trails before lunch and, of course, a midnight party for New Year's."

She reached for an appetizer and he couldn't read her expression, but her body tensed ever so slightly. "The ride is the part that involves the horses, I presume."

"Mmm-hmm."

She shrugged. "Sure. As long as I get to try my luck against the machines when we get back."

"You don't have to gamble to try your luck," he said, then stuck a strawberry in her mouth before she could respond.

"By the way, the New Year's party is a masquerade ball. They give out masks and all."

Her eyes lit up. "Cool."

Wanting to shake the damned shadows he'd somehow put in her eyes, he plopped a tiny dollop of cream on the tip of her nose. "Ah. Mental note. Masks are exciting. Horses, hoofs, and teeth, not so much."

"That's cruel!"

"It's cute."

She tried to wipe it with her hand, but he held it down, so she stuck her tongue out, but it didn't quite reach. The sight had his blood thickening, though.

He swooped down to kiss her, smearing the light cream between their faces. Her tongue flicked into his mouth, then out to lick his cheek, the velvet caress returning to the kiss with the taste of fresh cream.

He pulled her closer still and took his fill of her lips, belatedly reminding himself to take it slow.

"Eat," he ordered, pushing her away and turning her toward the food. "Build up your energy. You're going to need it."

She raised an eyebrow. "Promise?"

"Oh, you bet I do."

Tanika lay dizzy, weak, and breathless, unable to even open her eyes. Good God, that man could keep a promise.

He'd worked her thoroughly on the picnic towels. Moved the action to the bed for more. He'd taken her in the shower, slick with water and soap. And even when she'd bent over the sink, brushing her teeth, he'd been there.

She'd tried to dominate him in the bed, to take back some of the control she no longer felt she had, but he'd denied her, and subjected her to the longest, most torturous body licks she'd ever had to endure. Then he'd slid into her again, thick and deep and slow-paced, the contact made even more pleasurable because of her overly sensitive vagina.

He was ruthless with his tactics, until she finally writhed and begged for completion, until she'd had no choice, absolutely none at all, but to fall apart in his arms, surrendering her pleasure, her heart, her very soul . . .

His ejaculation seeped hot inside her, his rough exhale searing her lips. His heart thundered loudly against hers, his ribs were pressed against hers, his cock and thighs possessing her still.

"No more . . . please," she whispered weakly against his chin.

He pressed a gentle kiss against her forehead. "No more. Sleep," he murmured.

Cradling her head, he rolled her so that she was on her side, against him, limp as a cooked noodle.

He whispered her name, and she smiled as she dreamed . . .

chapter 10

Damon woke up reaching across the bed and ended up cussing. A peek at her pillow revealed a vast space of emptiness replaced by a note.

She'd left him a goddamned note! He rubbed his eyes with the palms of his hands, gritted his teeth and sighed. She was running scared and, hell, he wasn't sure he would change his approach even if he could.

He kicked the sheets off and stood before snatching the note to read her curly scratches.

I'm starved. I'll be at the breakfast buffet (or gambling). Call me when you wake up.

He crumpled the note and tossed it into the trash bin in the bathroom.

He had less than twelve hours to convince her that what they had was more than just a physical affair. At the very least, he hoped she'd consider extending their time together.

Instead, she was blocking his every turn.

Well, he wasn't giving up that easy.

Not without a fight.

Tanika fed the coin machine another ration of digital quarters and tried to drown out the ear-banging jangle of the machines around her. A headache had begun to germinate when she'd snuck out of the room and now threatened to become an eye-blinding hatchet-slamming throb on the side of her head.

This was better than fighting for the covers that always seemed to end up on his side of the bed. It wasn't normal to *want* to stick around and watch him grumble his way to the bathroom. Who wanted an audience when they shaved or brushed their teeth . . . although he had liked to watch her brush— but that was beside the point!

Yeah, this way was easier on her head and her heart.

Yet the jumble of emotions that had swamped her last night only fermented. In less than twelve hours, their relationship would be officially over.

As if conjured up by her thoughts, the gleam of Damon's head appeared as he moved through the crowd.

He found her easily and the path seemed to clear for him as he approached. He wore light blue jeans, a wheat-colored sweater that showed off all his brawn. Man, he already had her getting all breathy and weak in the knees.

Mine.

The single word sprung into her head and refused to budge. It lodged deeper when he greeted her, then bent his head and sucked the breath out of her in a devastating, mouth-tangling kiss.

"Good morning," he said gruffly.

"Mmm." Yes, it sure was. Why did it feel as if her heartbeat were pounding faster and yet slower at the same time?

"How's your luck going?" Damon asked Tanika.

"I win some, I lose some. Trying to quit while I'm ahead."

"Sometimes, it's worth the gamble." He held her gaze, until she was forced to look away, trying not to read too much into his words.

"Then again, sometimes it's not," she replied, pressing the necessary buttons to cash out. She'd been stupid enough to gamble her heart on love before and there had been no payoff then.

Never again.

Just like the measly coins that were noisily falling into the money tray, cashing out was the only smart thing to do. Gathering the coins, she put them into her purse.

Flashing a smile she didn't feel, she asked, "Where to?"

His smile looked a little strained, too. "Outdoors. To the sleigh ride, to commune with nature."

Too romantic, her heart thumped. "I'd rather commune with a really fast snowmobile."

He paused. "A snowmobile . . . Have you ever been on a snowmobile?"

"First time for everything, right? How difficult can it be?"

He shrugged. "Okay. Whatever the lady wants, the lady gets."

"Wow, you're easy."

He kissed her knuckles, murmuring, "You have no idea."

Twenty minutes later, Damon had purchased some snow gear and Tanika stepped out of the small store bundled in warm clothes, feeling like a snow bunny. On the other hand, Damon looked like a ski instructor.

She half listened when they were given instructions, and much too soon, she found herself racing Damon's snowmobile as he tore through the fresh snow.

The wind was brisk, the snow was as soft as down feathers, rounding out the landscape as they blazed past the branches and trunks of thick pine trees. At several points, she caught glimpses of the gunmetal-gray surface of the lake against an equally severe sky.

Part of her wanted to stop him and point to a landmark where in the summertime, horses could be rented for scenic trails. At another spot farther down, kayaks could be rented for the quiet bay.

For almost an hour, they circled the course, avoiding other snowmobiles and sailing up and down the slopes. This, she realized, she could handle. Having fun with him made time fly by and kept the looming future at bay.

Fun was the key.

After all, how could he break her heart if they were only having fun?

Oh, a New Year's Erotique ball," Tanika observed, pointing to a sign depicting masked seminude dancers in a ballroom. They had returned the snowmobiles and were hiking back to the hotel. But after seeing the flyer, Tanika stopped to read the details.

"Want to go? Sounds like it's going to be fun."

Damon shoved his hands into his pockets, bracing more against her comments than the lingering cold. "Actually, I'd planned to attend the dinner and symphony on their top floor."

"But." She raised her index finger to ward off his comments. "Wouldn't you rather wear a costume than a black bow tie tonight? Don't you want to try a nontraditional New Year's? Try something with pizzazz, passion, midnight inspirations . . . Something guaranteed to be fun!"

"I happen to think symphonic music is fun."

She blinked hard, and he was sure it was to cover up for the fact that she wanted to roll her eyes at his comment.

"Well . . . then." She glanced back at the sign. "Maybe we can go to both. This one starts early, so we could skip out in the middle and come back in time to attend the one upstairs."

He immediately thought of his parents and grandparents, and the years they'd spent returning to the same place to celebrate the New Year. Did it really matter if it was a long-standing family tradition as long as she was with him to celebrate the night?

"The Erotique ball it is," he said.

Her eyes beamed and she stood on her toes to kiss his cold lips. "Thanks!"

"More of that later. Right now I'm wondering how you're going to come up with two outfits for that freaky party in only a couple of hours."

"Oh, there's nothing I love more than a shopping challenge. Want me to pick yours or do you want to tag along?"

Shopping on New Year's Eve? Was she insane? "Um, no, thanks." He turned toward a nearby display window, mentally cringing at the prices. "By the look of these prices . . ."

Damon turned back around to nothing but air. Funny. The last time he'd checked, Tanika had been going through her tiny purse for credit cards, and now she was making a whirlwind path toward the hotel stores, barely remembering to wave at him before she disappeared into the throng of shoppers.

Damon cleared his throat, pretended he hadn't just been talking to himself, and headed back to the room.

* * *

    *T*he sun had just crested behind the mountains, bathing the vast lake and icy caps with poppy-orange hues that bled to the palest pink. It was the ultimate sunset for lovers, evidenced by the number of couples who had chosen to stop and admire it.

    "Angel wings?" Damon kept his eyes straight ahead but his tone said he was definitely not thrilled. He hadn't been since she'd showed up at the hotel room with the custom outfit for him.

    "I asked you if you wanted to shop with me—"

    "And somehow, you thought I'd like angel wings."

    Tanika briefly wished he'd take a couple of deep breaths and loosen up. "As you'd warned me, there were slim pickings."

    "Hmm."

    Frankly, when faced with the choices of angel wings or a flamboyant Little Richard costume, she thought she'd made the right decision.

    Besides, the more she'd thought about it, the more she realized that getting loud and wild at the Erotique ball would be just the thing she needed.

    "It's the perfect ensemble. I go as a naughty devil and you go as my guardian angel," she explained. "Besides, it was far better than the alternative, trust me."

    "How do I let you talk me into these things?" he muttered under his breath.

"Hmm. I could've asked you to wear the candy nipple rings," she said, glad to see his frown turn into a grin.

"Not a chance in hell. Speaking of which, please tell me you're wearing more than just a devilish thong and bra under that coat."

"That's all part of the surprise. Just keep in mind that it's only a party, and remember, this is supposed to be *fun*."

His skeptical expression was his only response.

When they arrived, they paid the entry fee at the door and followed the ghouls, goddesses, and a very thin guy in a toga. Even before they'd reached the front door, the music reached their ears, pumping hard as if attempting to leave the building.

It was hard to tell if the howling sounds were from animals in the house or simply part of the music. In the lobby, Damon reluctantly removed his coat to reveal his bare chest and white leather pants. Instead of a regular zipper in the front, there were hoops that held a leather tie in the event that he should want to expose himself at a moment's notice.

Jesus. He would never have purchased such an outfit even if someone had held a gun to his head. So how on earth had she talked him into wearing it?

She nudged him with the mini pitchfork. "Come on. Let me fluff up your wings just a bit."

Reluctantly, he turned and withstood the embarrassment while she angled out the wings that were attached to the vest in the back.

"There." She gave his shoulder a final tap, her fingers lingering on his spine. "I have to say, you look absolutely divine."

"Yeah, yeah." He tugged at her coat belt. "Now, let's see what you've got."

His heart came to a complete stop when Tanika slipped off her coat, revealing a tight cat-woman-type suit of leather. Tiny bursts of flames and a cleverly appliquéd devil's tail—in a vivid red satin—completed the outfit. On anyone else, the outfit would've seemed gaudy. On her it was positively devilish.

Two things became immediately apparent. First was that his leather jeans were quickly becoming too damned tight in the groin area. And secondly, that he was going to have to punch anyone who came on to her.

"Do you like it?"

Was the pope Catholic? Damon couldn't drag his eyes from the soft brown mounds of her breasts, and her lush revelation of cleavage! God, there was barely enough of the outfit to cover her essentials!

Sweet Lord, what a fine woman.

"Well?" There was the barest trace of apprehension in her voice.

Damon pulled her close and planted a possessive kiss on her mouth, stopping before he was forced to adjust himself or risk permanent damage to his tightly packed penis. "Next time, I'm not letting you out the door without seeing your outfit first."

She licked her lips, looking flustered and a little breathless. "Next time?"

He'd plain forgotten there would be no next time. Dammit, she would bring that up now?

He checked his wristwatch. "We leave in exactly an hour."

"You're carrying the angelic thing a little far, Damon."

"There's nothing angelic about it." One hour was going to be more than enough time to make some of the guys that were gawking at her go from foolish to stupid. Apparently, she didn't see that it meant he'd have to kick the stupid person's ass and the whole mess would likely end up with him in jail.

"One hour," he repeated. "Maybe even sooner."

"We'll see." She tried to move away from him, but he reeled her back in.

"I'm no angel, Tanika. Don't push me."

Understanding dawned in her eyes and she touched his cheek. "Okay. One hour."

The coat clerk gave them their tokens, handed Tanika a small pager that glowed green.

"What's that?" Damon asked.

"A, uh, delightful unexpected event."

"Is that a euphemism for 'surprise'?" Another one?

"Something like that. Don't look so worried," she

said, clipping the pager to the thin whip that was wrapped like a belt around her shapely hips.

"Right."

They moved through a small tunnel and emerged in a place that seemed to have no sky, scant clothes, and no rules. Like a bizarre painting, there were sections of the party that were cloaked in dark hues of bronze, purple, and black, while other places glimmered brightly, like rooms in a jeweled harem.

Saying the party had an erotic theme was an understatement, Damon realized. Dancers, naked but for glittering body paint and the merest thongs, moved in spotlit areas, undulating and gyrating in clusters or swinging from strategically placed trapezes.

The room was a mad crash of music and costumes, booze and bodies, contributing to the blatant sexual atmosphere. Neon blinking signs pointed to other provocative attractions.

Wacky Willie. Hole in the Wall. Amazing Craze.

Damon didn't even want to guess as to where the Pucker Up arrow led.

The urge to throw Tanika over his shoulder and bail for the door grew increasingly stronger.

"Here, have a brew," Tanika said, handing him a courtesy bottle and taking a pull from her own. "You should try to relax and look more angelic. I'm guessing angels don't give people the evil eye like you're doing."

"I'm trying to expand my 'traditional' mind."

She smiled. "How's that going?"

"I'm getting distracted by the men that are ogling you."

"They're not. If anything, compared to other women here, I'm overdressed."

He held his beer, unwilling to drink it. "They're drooling."

She peered over his shoulder. "Well, in that guy's defense, he has knuckles that are practically dragging on the ground. I think he would drool at the sight of wheat grass. Don't get your feathers all ruffled."

"Then tell me what the pager is for."

"It's a surprise. A special gift from me to you."

"Tanika—"

"Oh, look!" She held up the pager with a wicked grin on her face when the green glow of her unit turned red. "Come on. It's just a little private session I ordered up."

His gut twisted with apprehension. "I didn't come here to engage in private sessions."

The fact that she looked slightly nervous wasn't calming his nerves at all. "Damon, really. Would I do anything reckless?"

He warred with indecision, the low angel feathers at his back causing a ticklish effect as people walked behind him.

"I'm sure this is going to be a whole lot less exciting than you're probably imagining. Trust me," she said, tugging him along.

Reluctantly, he followed as she led the way to Ride the Pole where a Goth-dressed woman took her pager and led them to a private room.

The second they entered, the deafening blast of the party outside was minimized to a rhythmic bass that seemed to pound on the walls.

"Everything has been sterilized and will be cleaned again when you leave," their Goth guide explained, pointing out other things in the room to Tanika. "We hold firm to the time limits, though, so please use your time wisely."

Tanika and Damon were left alone, the door closing solidly behind their guide as she left.

Damon looked around the small room, noticing the "private dancer" stage, the steel pole, and the single seat in front of it all. There was a faint lingering smell of disinfectant that distracted from the moment.

"Okay, big boy," Tanika said, obviously going into a different role. "You heard the lady. I have to use the time wisely, so have a seat."

He widened his stance and stood his ground. "I prefer to stand."

She glanced at the bulge in his pants with a saucy grin. "I like it when you stand, too."

She sashayed her sweet behind to the stage in a way that made the leather pants shrink by the second.

She stopped by the audio equipment that the Goth had showed her, selected a song, and as the jazz-infused techno beat started up, she transformed before his eyes. Her head was down, her shoulders slumped and her eyes closed, but as the music swelled she seemed to blossom, pushing her shoulders back, arching her spine and opening her eyes.

Only for him.

It dawned on him that she was like a hit of her own perfume . . . with a single inhalation of her scent, she could easily send him into another frame of mind, haunting him. Watching her dance was like drinking in the heat of her passionate kisses with his eyes.

She moved, stepping closer to the pole, her body seeming to control the music rather than the other way around. With her hands above her head, she gripped the pole and did an amazing split maneuver that swung her around in an arch to land on the floor like a gymnast.

When had she learned to do that?

She whipped back up and wrapped a long leg around the pole, dipping back and showing enough flexibility to make him wide-eyed and slack-jawed. Sweet Moses . . .

His cock strained painfully in his pants and he exhaled, the shimmer of feathers tickling his back. She seduced him with the language of sinuous shifts of her hips, with the roll and curve of her butt, and the subtle sway of her leather bustier.

Her high-heeled boots nailed each step she took down the short runway, stomping up his pulse until he was forced to ease the laces over his groin.

He walked up the steps to the stage, not waiting for the music to stop. In the back of his mind, a voice warned that there could be camera equipment filming their every move, and yet it didn't stop him from trapping her with her back to the pole and kissing the hell out of her.

He wanted to grind his hips into hers, wanted to be inside her, knowing it could take very little to push him over the edge. She moaned, the sound all husky and womanly with need. Her breath was already shallow and her skin gleamed from her vibrant dancing.

He ran his hands restlessly over her torso, frustrated that he couldn't get to her through all the straps of satin and leather.

Even as he devoured her mouth, he was able to slide his hand deep down the front of her pants, her thighs parting to accommodate his fingers until his fingertips were wet with her arousal. Her clitoris was a semifirm nub firmly under the pad of his middle finger and he stroked it gently, delving to the opening of her folds and feeling her surrender to every subtle nuance of his touch.

"Ah, oh, oh . . . fuck . . . Damon . . . my God."

He sucked on the pulse of her neck, the muscles of his arm burning with the control it took to stroke the tight space between her thighs and the leather.

He waited for it, almost coming himself when he heard her shuddered breath start to break, her arms clutching him as she arched into the orgasm. Beneath his finger, her clit throbbed and it gave him supreme satisfaction knowing she was peaking beneath his touch.

His cock throbbed painfully, seeking release, but Damon gritted his teeth, barely holding the urges at bay. In his mind's eye, it was easy to imagine what they'd look like, an angel submitting to the lust of a devil. Or was it the other way around?

Suddenly a flash of red from the corner of the room drew his attention and he looked up to see a sign that warned they had thirty seconds left.

He tried to withdraw his hand but Tanika gasped. "Hold on just a minute—"

"No, we're out of time." He felt like he was thirty seconds from his dick exploding. He would've given anything for more privacy.

As the flashing clock wound down to fifteen seconds, he stepped away from her, seeing her puffy lips, her mouth all soft and inviting, her body weak and replete.

She licked her lips, and for a heated moment, he fantasized them parting for his erection, yearning to feel that slickness of her mouth surrounding his cock, to have the barest graze of her teeth and the stroke of her velvet tongue coax the last of his come into the very depths of her kiss.

Her knowing eyes locked with his. "I'm sorry. I should've planned this better."

A buzzer sounded and they moved farther apart just as the doors opened. A man, dressed like a janitor, walked in with a bucket, several spray bottles and small towels in his hand. He ignored them and went right to wiping down the stainless steel chair Damon had not even sat in.

Tanika straightened, shaking a little. Moving closer to her, he adjusted the laces over his groin and pulled her toward the exit, his body in agony. "Let's get out of here."

chapter 11

No sooner had they stepped out than the blast of chaos surrounded them again. Not far from the exit, a throng of people had gathered around a spotlight, and one of the talented balletlike dancers ran among the crowd, pretending to tug at a person only to turn away at the last minute.

Damon skirted them, pushing a path outward, but was spun around. The masked woman ran and jumped up, wrapping her legs around his hips and holding tight.

Damon stumbled backward, barely managing to grip a nearby steel bar and not fall. And in the two seconds it took him to recover, a door closed before him and he found himself trapped in a man-sized birdcage that was being steadily elevated over the crowd, moving toward an unknown destination.

"Damon!"

Tanika's shout was drowned in the cheers and hoots of the crowd. Damon's captor extracted herself long enough to pirouette around him, doing a lascivious dance and raking in more cheers from the crowd below.

"I caught myself a well-hung bird," she shouted, dancing away and groping his butt, then darting away again.

It was all Damon could do not to cover his crotch. It was bad enough that he was trussed up with wings, but being in the spotlight with a painfully hard erection was more than enough.

He grabbed the woman and growled to her face, "Set this thing down right now."

"Oh, honey, don't get mad. It's just some—"

"Now!"

Behind her mask, her eyes narrowed. "Are you gonna make me? Oh, please, say you will . . . I've been so bad . . ."

He pushed her away, muttering a profanity. He looked through the bars at the view below, searching for Tanika. The bird's-eye view revealed an old English hedge maze where he saw one woman bound to the center of a flowing fountain while behind her a man was busy paddling her behind.

He could hear her moan and the fleshy slap each time the paddle made contact with her skin. He turned away to see a cluster of people in the darker corners of a dead end, writhing and grappling with each other, obviously in the throes of sex.

The purpose of the Hole in the Wall was apparent from where he stood. On one side, men thrust their eager cocks through mouth-sized holes in the walls while on the other side, a kneeling body with an eager mouth took it in.

The sounds of sex and need wafted up to his ears, surrounding him like a drugging fog, repelling more than intriguing him.

He caught glimpse of a devilish outfit turning a corner and his heart lunged in his chest.

Tanika!

She disappeared.

"Last chance, lady," he said to the woman who was still mindlessly prancing around the unsteady cage. "Either open the door now or I'm kicking it down."

She practically plastered herself on him, grinding her hips against his. "Why don't we show the crowd how it's really done, huh?"

She cupped his crotch and began to massage him, but he pulled her hand away, anger making his grip stronger than he'd intended. She seemed to enjoy it.

"I guess I do this the hard way, then," he snarled. Pushing her aside, he aimed a hard kick on the locked cage door and it burst open, hanging noisily on its hinges, at least fifteen feet from the ground.

He peered down and spotted three haystacks. The masked woman called out to him as he took a flying leap and landed onto the soft pile, rolling down to the bottom.

The damned angel wings crunched under his back, the hay poked and tickled his exposed skin, and to his dismay, he realized he'd landed just a few feet away from where two cowboy boots in a nearby horse stall were set in a position that could only mean one thing. Sex.

Damon dusted off, averted his gaze, and spotted the sign above the entryway. THE ROLL IN THE HAY STABLE.

This was Tanika's idea of fun?

Fed up and frustrated, Damon tossed off the angel wings and stalked out, wincing at each step because of his erection and glad that it was finally starting to soften. Not by much.

Truth be told, he wasn't sure what to make of the party, but if this was who she really was, he wasn't sure he could deal with it.

After five minutes of roaming around without a clue as to where he was heading, Damon finally stopped at a tattoo booth and, over the flank of a man who was getting a snarling ape tacked on his butt, got instructions to the front entrance of the party.

He was heading into familiar territory when he heard the blood-curdling scream followed by a loud splash. Heart pounding, he raced toward the sound that could only be Tanika's voice.

He turned the corner and found her in the "Goo Gun Shooting Gallery." Someone had pointed a phallic-shaped gun at her and fired the gooey liquid on her back and some of her chest. She was now glaring at the idiot like she was about to slaughter him.

The man dropped the goo gun and bolted, leaving her with her hands on her hips and a slew of curses blistering the air.

Damon found himself grinning, feeling much happier than moments before. He strode toward her, stopping a few feet away.

"And here I thought you'd be lost without me," he said, "or worse, having fun."

She whirled around and her anger faded into a quick, bright smile. "Oh, thank God you made it down. Would you mind waiting just a minute longer while I go hunt that bastard and shove his goo gun where it belongs?"

"What'd he do?"

"He told me the birdcage controller was through that door over there, then when I went there, he tagged me with this crap."

She huffed, her lovely hairdo reduced to limp, curly strands that sat like a mop on her head. "Do you have any idea how much this outfit cost? Did I look like I wanted to ruin it with . . . whatever the hell this is."

Knowing that no one would stare at her now, Damon smiled broadly. "Want me to hunt him down for you? I could hold him down while you get a couple of good punches in."

This time, her face lit up like sunshine.

"Very tempting. And not very angelic of you, either. By the way, what happened to your wings?"

He shrugged. "If they're no good when jumping

from high places, why keep them? Where's your pitchfork?"

She mimicked his shrug and it made him just want to kiss her.

"Okay, goo-woman, had enough?" he asked.

"Goo-woman?" When she inhaled like that, her breasts almost heaved out of her leather bra.

"I mean that in the most flattering way possible. It puts a fine shine on your exceptional cleavage and also draws the eyes to your fine behind, which I should mention I've wanted to sink my teeth into all night."

Her eyebrows went up, her chin jutted out, and she ruthlessly managed to keep a smile from her lips. "You're a lousy suck-up but amazingly, right now, I'll take each and every compliment."

"Perfect. Then how about we quit this place?"

"Absolutely."

He winked, took her hand, and led the way back toward the front door, where he was able to convince one of the employees to let him use their showering facilities. Damon guarded the shower stall while Tanika washed off the "goo."

He was waiting patiently when she tapped on the door and peered out.

"Could you please get me my coat?"

"Your coat?"

"I can't wear this again, it's just covered with this stuff and it won't wash off this outfit."

It seemed to take a second longer for him to get her point. "So, you're just going to wear the coat?"

"You're enjoying this, aren't you?"

"Not nearly as much as I should. Lock the door. I'll be right back."

He returned wearing his own coat and tapped on the door to hand her hers. He guarded the door again and a few minutes later, they left.

Damon couldn't help thinking that she'd transformed, like a superhero returning to her normal clothes. Her rinsed hair was in a lovely conservative knot again, and her boots clicked sturdily against the sidewalk. The plastic bag of soiled clothes was at her side like a briefcase. Her makeup was all but gone and the result was a whole new refreshing appearance.

Suddenly Damon was more than a little annoyed with himself, for not being able to control his reaction to her even when she was at her worst. Or at her best.

Or, frankly, ever.

chapter 12

*T*anika clutched her wet clothes in the plastic bag and held her coat tightly closed around her, as much for heat as to cover her complete nakedness beneath it. Damon, thank God, seemed to be lost in his own thoughts.

Well, her idea of a fun evening had certainly gone wrong. She'd probably embarrassed him, showed him a rotten time, and still he'd escorted her as politely as if he were wearing a tuxedo and she an evening gown.

It must've been the trembling that caused him to wrap one of his strong arms around her shoulders, pulling her to his side. Then with his other hand, he dug out his mobile phone to call the hotel and request that they draw a bath for her in their room.

Emotion welled inside her, tightening her chest in a bittersweet grip. She brushed her lips against his cheek in thanks, but avoided making eye contact the entire way back to the hotel.

It wasn't guilt, she assured herself. Nor disappointment. And under no circumstances was it anything as complicated as love.

They reached the hotel in comfortable silence, winding their way toward the elevators among people wearing glimmering ball gowns and crisp tuxedoes. Some were already sporting their elaborate evening masks.

Back in their hotel room, Tanika worked off her boots and immediately headed for the prepared, sudsy bathtub, Damon not far behind.

"I'm sorry about the way the evening turned out," she said, watching his hands lather up soap.

"The evening isn't over yet."

"Yes, but—"

He kissed her, nipping and tonguing her until she heard her own moan echoing around her. His hands chased the wash of water on her body.

"Thanks was for the private-dancer gift," he said, his voice already getting gravelly.

She rubbed the soap around his chest, her nipples so sensitive against his chest hair. "You're welcome."

"Now I have a gift for you, too."

"It wouldn't happen to be poking at my belly right now, would it?" she asked, her hand moving down to stroke his jutting cock.

His chuckle was dry, almost pained, as he pulled her hand away. "No, no. I'm not going to rush this."

"Rush it if you want. I'm not complaining."

"I'm thinking it's delving time again." He kissed her again, slowly, as if she were a flavor that kept changing on his tongue.

"What are you in the mood for?" she asked when she surfaced for gulps of air.

"The ND Tantric Sex Manual." He nibbled the corner of her mouth, his hands cupping her breasts while his cock pushed thick and hard against her hip.

"Tantric?" Of all the products, that manual was one she'd glanced through but not read in much detail. "As in meditation?"

"We can bend the rules a little."

He stopped her oncoming questions with more kisses, and moments later, she was carefully grinding her hips over his shaft, taking him in circular, smooth, nerve-tingling moves.

He gritted his teeth and held his eyes tightly shut for a few long seconds. His hands squeezing her hips kept her immobile when she wanted nothing more than to rock on him. Water lapped around them like music.

"Breathe with me," he said gruffly.

Breathe? Who could breathe when she was panting like a dog in heat?

Beneath her, he studied her through half-open eyes, all the while taking deep long breaths. She tried to imitate him, but no amount of breathing could divert her mind from the sheer fullness of him inside her.

He took her hands and put them on her thighs. "Close your eyes, look at the ceiling and breathe."

She tried it, much too aware that her breasts were aching, swaying in the water. The steamy air and Damon's deep kisses were making her a little light-headed.

Warm water caressed her everywhere when he moved his large hands to her knees, then upward.

"Breathe . . ."

His fingers spread out as he reached the apex of her thighs, and his thumbs came together ever so perfectly over her clitoris.

"Ah . . . Damon . . . " Water sloshed quietly.

"Breathe."

She stared blindly up at the white ceiling, feeling the roll of his thumbs caress her clit again, separate the delicate, petal-like labia, and do the whole thing all over again.

Her hands clenched against her thighs and she ground her hips down against his touch, forgetting to breathe as a wet wave of sensation trembled in her womb.

She heard his half-broken murmured words, could feel the thick hardness of him that seemed to get harder as she got wetter. A restless stillness grew and blossomed with every touch of his thumbs. The dual movements stripped her senses, overrode them to the point that she could only keep the orgasm at bay by breathing his way.

"Be still. Wait, hold it . . ."

She wasn't aware when she stopped looking at the ceiling. She just knew that she was looking at his straining face, at the vein in his neck, then into the pools of his eyes, and knew she was going under.

The orgasm swamped her, spasming from his thumbs straight into her through her clit, stealing her breath and shivering on her skin, outside and in.

"Oh!"

She felt like a machine whose components had exploded. Catching her breath now only seemed to fit him in deeper, and as the dizziness swarmed her, she felt his hot release shooting deep inside her womb.

She slumped over his chest, not sure if he was riding her or she was riding him. Struggling to breathe, she laid her head on his chest, the soft water and remaining bubbles making it a slippery pillow.

As her breathing settled, she snuggled closer, feeling his arms around her, and rested on him with her eyes closed.

Almost an hour later, Damon fought the weariness and carried Tanika to the bed. He'd shifted her to his side, and was content enough to watch her sleeping, afraid that if he too fell asleep, he'd wake up empty-handed again.

But in the end, he intended to close his eyes for just a moment, and must've dozed, waking only when he felt Tanika rolling away from him.

His arms automatically tightened around her, and when he opened his eyes, she looked like a deer caught in the headlights.

"Where are you going?" he grumbled, still not completely awake.

There was a pause, then her hand came up to leisurely trace a path on his chest. "The party starts in an hour. I need to get dolled up for it. You know, makeup, hair and that kind of thing."

"Honey"—he tugged at her hand—"you're too beautiful to need a whole hour for that."

She chuckled, a sweet soft sound that thrilled him even as she tugged her hand free. "Said like a man who still wants some."

"Hey, even I need some downtime."

"Well, you relax while I get ready."

He watched her cover up with a robe as she went to the bathroom without once glancing back at him. His right arm still tingled, recovering from the numbness when she'd been sleeping against it. He wouldn't mind having that feeling again . . .

He sat up in the bed and, out of habit, checked his wristwatch. Two hours left till the end of the year, till the end of what they had.

Had the affair honestly been only a fling to her?

Damon rubbed his temples, stretched, then wrapped a bedsheet around his hips. He lumbered over to his laptop just as she started the shower.

His digital camera was still hooked up, so he

reviewed the photos he'd taken of her, moving frame by frame, the memory of each picture coming alive.

In some, her eyes gleamed with invitation. He loved the curve of her lips, too. And her posture said more than words.

He paused on the picture where her eyes had widened and that flustered expression had been clear. A few had captured the panic dawning on her. Not fear, but something bordering on it, and yet . . . he couldn't quite decipher it.

He studied them a while longer before moving on.

The photos she'd taken of him were also very interesting. Always little pieces of him. His toes. Then part of his hand. His elbow. His chin, jaw, and ear. Little pieces, but not the whole face, arm, or for that matter, foot.

Interesting. Maybe she could only handle a little at a time.

It didn't explain why she'd centered the picture of him covering himself with the bedsheet. That was the only shot she'd taken that spanned his chest, arms, hips, and part of his thighs. On the other hand, maybe that picture in particular said it all. Maybe that was the only part of him she wanted. His dick.

He rubbed his hands over his face, then turned toward the sound of running water. Women. Inexplicable and forever intriguing.

He reached for his cell phone and called the other intriguing woman in his life.

"Happy New Year, Nana," he said when she picked up.

"Damon! Happy New Year to you. How's Tahoe?"

"Lovely any time of year. By the looks of things out my window, the partying has already started."

"Same over here. Lola and Cassandra are here and we're all sipping some truly horrible soy hot chocolate, and watching the revelers on TV."

He chuckled because he could hear her slurping her drink and was willing to bet there was nothing soy about it.

"Well, please tell them happy New Year for me."

"Sure will. I hope you're enjoying the room . . . with a special someone?"

"The room is great."

"And the special someone?"

"Is currently taking a shower."

"Ah." But the single word was filled with smugness. "Don't let me keep you, then."

"You're not." He fought not to exhale into the phone. "Just wanted to say New Year's won't be the same without you . . . but I'll be thinking of you and hope you have a great time."

His grandmother made a familiar mothering sound. "She must be something special if you took her up there."

He smiled to himself. "We're just here to enjoy the fireworks."

"And I'm over here enjoying hot cocoa."

He rubbed his jaw. "Touché."

She chuckled. "You know, traditionally, New Year's is a great way to start things off romantically."

He was so startled, he coughed. "What exactly did you mix into your cocoa?"

"A little of this and a little of that. It's making me nostalgic, to tell you the truth."

Sounded more like tipsy to him. He bit back a lecture on mixing medication and alcohol.

"Edna brought the latest pictures of her grandson. Cute as a button with an Afro that won't quit." She chuckled. "So precious."

He heard the sadness and longing that lingered in her voice, and something twisted inside him.

"Love," she added, "brings with it so many wonderful and amazing gifts. I wish that for you, Damon. Because once you know love, you can't mistake it for anything else . . ."

"Nana—"

"It's just that you're so organized, so busy! So focused on your career, or the perfect image and all. I worry that you'll blink and miss it, baby."

What the hell was she drinking?

"But listen to me, just carrying on. Maybe I will lay off the, um, cocoa."

"That would ease my mind greatly."

She laughed. "I worry about you, is all. Now, have yourself a great New Year's, okay?"

They said their goodbyes and he hung up, feeling completely confused.

• • •

Later, when Damon was in the shower, Tanika stopped drying her hair long enough to answer her cell phone.

"Hey, sis!" Cindy's voice boomed in her ear; she was obviously at a crowded party. "Happy New Year!"

"Hey, girl! Back at ya!"

"I'm kicking it at Mark and Jody's. You know, they have the eats on the grill, the wine flowing, and the music thumpin' . . . What about you?"

"I'm getting all dolled up to go to the ball." *Not to mention preparing myself for a breakup.*

"Cool. Well, I wanted to say happy New Year just in case things got crazy and I ran out of time . . . and you know, about the other night . . . I just wanted to say that my New Year's resolution is to not give you crap on how you lead your love life. I mean, you have a plan that works for you. And who knows? It takes all kinds to make this world go around. So, hey, if that's the way you want it, then, you go for it! I didn't want to end the year on a bad note."

Tanika sat at the edge of the bed. "You're still dwelling on that? I'd forgotten all about it."

"I just worry about you, sis. But like you said, you're a big girl and you know what you're doing, so . . . Hugs from all of us and happy New Year!"

By the time Tanika finally hung up the phone, she wanted nothing more than to wind the clock back and start the whole affair over again.

Her fingers hovered over the number pad, as she hesitated to call her sister back and tell her she couldn't relate to any of those declarations of sexual liberation she'd been so vehement about in the past.

Six months ago, she would've been able to spout off her breakup lines without a hitch. Except lines like "Let's be friends" weren't going to cut it with Damon.

But, Christ, that was the bare truth! After tonight, it *was* going to be over, so the most logical thing to do would be to ignore the growing heartache and stick to her plan.

Leaving him would be quick and initially painful, but she'd get over it. She'd just have to think of it as ripping off a Band-Aid. Or duct tape.

The pain would eventually recede.

It had to.

chapter 13

An hour and a half later, Damon entered the ballroom with Tanika on his arm. She was so stunning in her gown, he almost didn't want to share her with the crowd. When he'd first set eyes on her, in their room, the thought that had crossed his mind was that she looked like a modern bride in that slim-fitting pale blue gown.

He'd simply watched her while he wrestled with the need to walk over, kiss her, and pour out his thoughts. But she'd been fussing with her hair and had smiled almost shyly at him from her reflection in the mirror.

And now, here he was, unable to hold down the feeling that he was about to give the bride away.

The glimmering lights from the chandeliers glowed warmly against the backdrop of a cerulean ceiling. On a small rotating stage, a cellist was so engrossed in playing his instrument, he seemed to be both embracing it and slow-dancing with it.

Damon took two glasses of champagne from a passing waiter and handed her one. Together they moved through the crowd while he greeted friends and old family acquaintances.

It was sheer torture to dance with her. Like a first dance at a wedding . . .

Every minute passed by like a slow-motion movie.

Tanika laughed at his friends' jokes, teased, and made interesting conversation that he somehow managed to follow. Every now and then, she'd grab a canapé from a passing waiter and hand it to him before taking one for herself.

Damon had no idea whether he ate gravel or caviar. The masks, the pretentious laughter, and the swell of classical music were starting to give him the surreal feeling of being trapped in a circus.

The large clock on the wall began to clang, warning of the fifteen minutes left until midnight.

He offered his hand. "Another dance?"

She nodded, and soon they had blended in with the crowd of dancers, pushed even closer by the throng.

"Almost midnight," he said. "It's such a beautiful night. It doesn't have to be about breakups. We could give ourselves a little more time."

He thought her breath hitched but wasn't sure. She angled her face closer to his cheek so he couldn't read her expression.

It seemed like forever before she replied. "Why postpone the inevitable, Damon? It was fun while it lasted, but we agreed to this, right? So let me make this easy for you. After tonight, it's back to professional business between us."

Her words blunted and numbed him. His feet refused to move, and there in the middle of the crowded dance floor, she finally looked up at him. "Out with the old, in with the new, right? Or something like that."

He remembered his words from earlier, when he'd been trying to be nonchalant about it. "You're so practical."

"I'm trying to be." Her eyes lowered, twisting him up even more. "It's what I want. What we both want, really."

"Is it?"

"Yes." This time, when she looked at him, her eyes gleamed with moisture, yet were filled with defiance. "Let's finish the dance," she whispered.

It took several seconds for her words to process, but then he began moving without thought, twirling her through the swarm of dancers, and feeling the seconds sucking him toward midnight, tearing jagged holes into his soul.

He didn't want to stop dancing, didn't want to face fireworks that would remind him of another time and place with her. But when the lights flickered dramatically and the confetti floated down like snow from the ceiling, he gave in to a last-minute, soul-searing impulse and pulled her in.

"Happy New Year," he said, then simply took the kiss, pouring his broken emotions into it, teeth scraping and tongues mingling. She responded by cupping his head in her hands and kissing him back with equal fervor. Off in the distance, the cannon-like boom of fireworks blasted the night.

When the kiss finally ended, they stared at each other for a stunned full second before someone spun her away, shouting, "Happy New Year." In an instant, he was pulled into a woman's arms, too, into a sea of people who were hugging and kissing and cheering like jackpot winners. The fireworks deafened the night sky, blitzing it with colors.

Crystal glasses were clicked together and champagne was sipped in a toast.

The crowd began to sing "Auld Lang Syne" as if a maestro had cued them, but Damon searched for Tanika, spotting her at the edge of the room, escaping like a modern Cinderella.

It's what I want, she'd said.

A slight pain drew his gaze to his hand, where he saw he'd snapped his champagne glass in two.

She was gone. Damon left the party only to encounter an empty hotel room.

He mentally tried to block out the words again, but they echoed in the room, reminders of her everywhere. Like the room, she'd left her mark in him, strewn memories all over his mind, scarring him with the erotic scents that were solely hers, of the lingerie that could never be worn by another woman.

And it was worse than her leaving his bed when he slept. Much worse than sitting up all night and studying the pictures she had taken or even having to sleep in a bed that still held her essence.

And definitely far worse than leaning his forehead against the door for half an hour, holding the doorknob and talking himself out of searching the hotel for her.

In the end, he packed his luggage, brewed some coffee, and waited until the sun painted the mountains with the luster of dawn. Sunlight on her skin probably looked a hell of a lot better than the view.

At almost six in the morning, Tanika attempted to sneak in, carefully opening the door and taking two steps into the room before realizing that he was sitting on the couch, waiting.

"I—I didn't want to wake you," she stammered.

"I'm awake." He forced himself to swallow the tepid coffee.

She looked around the room, her features tensing when she spotted his luggage. "Leaving?"

He shrugged. "I can wait for you if you like."

She tucked a stray curl behind her ear. "That would be nice. Thank you." So polite. And yet she smelled of alcohol and smoke, and the tired, guarded look in her eyes could be the result of . . . anything.

"Mind if I take a shower?" she asked.

Why do you need one? Too much sex? "Go ahead." It was as if the room had become a bullring, needing only the slightest provocation for a fight. She took a brief, short shower and returned to the room dressed conservatively in a warm cream-colored sweater and dark brown jeans.

Absolutely everything had changed.

She'd stayed up all night gambling, first at the roulette table, then when she'd won a reasonable sum, she'd moved to the coin-slot machines and played until she'd lost all her winnings.

Almost at the crack of dawn, she'd headed to the hotel room, sneaking in like a thief only to find Damon lurking like a dark angel in the shadows.

She'd wondered if he'd just walked in too and if so, from where. Another woman's bed?

No, Damon was solid. Dependable. Traditional. He'd take his time finding another lover. He probably wouldn't be impulsive again. Not like he'd been with her . . .

Now, Tanika was enduring the strained car trip by doing her best to ignore the tension that emanated from Damon.

Frustrated by her circling thoughts, Tanika reached into the back seat for her laptop computer and logged on until the wireless connection simply became too unstable to work. The radio was on, a mellow sound in the background that didn't dispel the lack of conversation.

Damon didn't bother with small talk. He had

dressed casually in a black turtleneck, navy jeans, and a matching jacket. The effect, along with his lightly tinted sunglasses, made him look like a brooding hit man.

In another place and time, she knew she'd be asking him to pull over to a secluded spot and let him into her steaming undies.

She'd make him keep his sunglasses on, too. Hell, she'd even call him "sir" again. And in the torrid fantasy, they'd grapple in the back seat and test the suspension of the sports-utility vehicle until they both needed a cigarette. Or a big fat Cuban cigar.

The alternative—to sit and watch the frosty winter scenery fly by—was more gut-wrenching.

She absently followed the weather report as it announced snowstorms in the foothills. Despite the density of the white clouds, the skies looked harmless enough.

"Would you like the heater on?" Damon asked when she crossed her legs.

How polite. "No, thank you."

She straightened the crease of her jeans, wanting to ask about his plans for his new boat, about masks, angel feathers, or the significance of early morning goodbyes. About anything, really, that would get the brooding expression off his face.

"So," she finally grumbled, "how about them Yankees?"

His lips moved into a quiet smile. "I'm more of a football fan."

Great. "Hmm."

For a moment, nothing was said.

"So, how about them Raiders?"

He glanced briefly at her. "When did you become a sports fanatic?"

"Hey, I'm just trying to spark up a conversation."

He shrugged in a way that told her absolutely nothing. "If you'll excuse me, I'm not in the mood for small talk. Not that I mind conversation, but if it's okay with you, I have things to think about."

That hurt, damn him. To be dismissed in such a blasé manner cut to the bone.

"Okay." She shrugged in turn and eased back her seat.

No. She would *not* dwell on it. Absolutely not. They were not even friendly strangers now. Barely even acquaintances. And she had no one to blame but herself.

Tanika realized she was rubbing her chest as if she could rub out the tight ache that continued to swell there. Holding back a sigh, she tucked her hands into her lap and stared out the window.

With the vents keeping her warm and the soft music on the radio, she was soon lulled into a sleepy coziness.

An hour later, the storm hit like a fist into a bag of flour, throwing whiteness everywhere. As the visibility got worse, Damon carefully tracked the radio's weather reports. Tanika was fast asleep and barely stirred when he had to pull over to have chains put on the tires.

When he got back into the car, she'd turned the radio up, a scowl on her face. "They just put up a roadblock."

The emergency broadcast repeated, and Damon mentally juggled his alternatives.

"Does this mean we head back?" Tanika asked.

"Let me ask around." He left the relative heat of the car to head back through snow that was ruining his shoes. He paid the mechanic who had put on his chains, but the conversation with him only confirmed what he already knew.

Moving to the nearby coffee hut, he spent an inordinate amount of money on two steaming cups of coffee and headed back to the car.

He set the coffees down in the cup holders and settled behind the wheel. "Looks like we're going to have to go with a contingency plan."

"Sounds serious."

"The storm has to blow over. It's going to take them hours to clear the roads and lift the roadblock, and the storm is not in full swing yet. It's very likely that if we try to move on, we could easily end up stuck in traffic for more than four hours."

She looked wide awake now. "So what now?"

"I'll have to backtrack for a couple of miles, but I know a place where we could wait out the storm."

Her face slackened. "You just happen to know of a place?"

"Yes."

"Are there any motels nearby?"

"No."

Her lips pursed. "Are we playing twenty questions and you never mentioned it?"

He popped the lid off his coffee and took a much-needed gulp of the steaming liquid. "A family friend has a rustic cabin that I borrow every now and then. It will hold us for a while."

She paused. "Please tell me it has an indoor bathroom."

"Yes. Still in working order, too."

Cupping her coffee in both hands, she watched him over the steam. "I have to warn you. I've never done rustic before."

"Well . . ." He'd never done full-bore heartache before, either. "Compared to hypothermia, it's not so bad, really."

"Good point."

She blew on her coffee and he had the urge to drag her onto his lap and kiss her with a fierceness that was almost overwhelming. Mentally muttering curses, he kept his hands firmly on the steering wheel, and turned his eyes back to the icy road.

Much later, Tanika stared into the snowy darkness to where the headlights illuminated a shack.

Not a cabin, but a shack. No one in their right

mind would call that collection of slapped-together lumber a cabin.

"It looks better from the inside," Damon assured her.

But after braving the slushy wind to get into the decrepit building, she realized the inside wasn't that much of an improvement. It was a *shack* that looked like it belonged in a bayou!

Damon used a flashlight he'd found in his car to illuminate the interior, showing furniture that was covered with sheets and corners laced with spiderwebs the size of windows.

Suddenly, being stuck on the freeway for an eternity didn't look so bad.

Damon walked around the small room, coming up with matches and then lighting lamps to reveal a stone woodstove, a small kitchen on one side, and a door that she hoped led to the restroom.

It was as if she'd landed back in the days of the Wild West. He pulled off the dusty sheets that covered a wooden couch, a bench, and a dinner table. In the corner, a queen-size bed was sealed in what appeared to be a huge plastic bag. Some woven rugs covered the floor and a few clay-and-feather art pieces decorated the walls.

The wind didn't howl through the building, so that at least indicated that it was solid. He walked to the cupboards, loudly opening and closing them, then the drawers.

"Just in case there are some critters around," he explained.

"Oh, great."

He left again and returned with the luggage, dropping them on the floor and shaking off the cold snowflakes from his jacket. He dug into one of his duffel bags and came up with some boots. He worked off his running shoes and put on the boots.

"What are you doing?" she asked when he began to rummage under the bed.

"I've got to get the generator started and I'd rather not freeze to death."

"Oh. Do you need help?"

"No, thanks. Just stay here and I'll be back."

With the boots on, he promptly headed out the door.

Tanika rubbed her cold arms. "Okay, then!"

The place needed a definite cleaning and something to clear out the musty smells. She dug through her overnight bag, glad that she usually packed a couple of extra outfits. The slimming gown wasn't going to do her any good, but the pink cashmere sweater and tweed oatmeal-colored pants would be warmer than what she was wearing.

She dressed quickly, hearing some light banging from the other side of the kitchen wall. Rolling up her sleeves, she found a broom and began to tear down the cobwebs and sweep the floor.

It was small. And cozy. With only one bed. She rubbed her forehead. How on earth were they going to pretend they hadn't been lovers? It was one thing to see him at work for a few hours a day and another to have to spend time with him this way. If they'd had one more day before the breakup, she could probably have handled this much better . . .

No, no, no!

She stopped her vigorous dusting to stare at the table, taken aback by the tiny voice in her head that was chanting "Yes!" even louder.

What had happened to her dignity? To sticking to the rules they'd made? Getting snowed in wasn't really a reason to resume sex for a day. Or two. Or God knew how long.

Christ!

In truth, resuming the affair was probably the sanest way to deal with the situation without falling completely apart. It was one more chance to have him and still keep her love locked quietly inside her.

She exhaled shakily, the thought circling with unbreakable logic.

She shook her head and resumed the cleaning.

Would it really be that bad to backtrack at this point? But wouldn't he be opposed to the idea?

She looked around the room. It was practically a honeymoon getaway. A very rustic, crude, and dusty one, but nonetheless . . . Maybe he'd picked it on purpose.

Or maybe she was grasping at straws!

She cleaned some more, talking herself in and out of the idea several times.

It wasn't until she found herself looking in her travel bag for the ND lavender and lemongrass candles that she realized she was going to go through with it.

"Good God. What am I doing?"

She had just lit two of the lavender- and lemongrass-scented tea lights, when she saw a furry movement from the corner of her eye.

Damon flinched and almost knocked his head against an overhead beam when he heard the blood-curdling scream. Even the hum of the generator that had just sprung to life, not to mention the wailing blizzard outside, hadn't dampened its volume.

He dropped everything and raced into the cabin to find Tanika standing on the kitchen table, the broom held over her head and a wild look in her eyes.

"There's a-a-a thing over there!" She pointed with the broom.

"Are you okay? Over where? What was it?"

She balanced in her mauve high-heeled boots and he absently wondered how she'd gotten up there with those heels on.

"It was a ball of fur! It ran into the corner and disappeared."

"Tanika, please get down before you break your neck."

"You didn't tell me there were rats!"

"We don't know it was—"

"It was a rat!"

He lowered her broom. "It could've been a mouse."

"Damon!"

"Okay, okay. See, it's gone." He looked around the room as if that were proof enough. "Let me finish with the generator and I'll see if I can hunt it down."

She started to step off the table when the broom fell with a thud to the floor. In a blink, she'd climbed halfway up his body, her face dangerously close to his as she strangled on a screech. He could even smell her peppermint gum.

"You have a fear of rats, I take it?"

With her teeth clenched, she growled. "So help me, you are *not* going to make a joke out of this!"

He knew better than to grin. "I never joke when I have heels digging into my butt."

Her chin went up, her eyes darkened slightly, and for a moment, he almost kissed her. His goddamned, traitorous penis started to swell and nudge against her like a dog looking to be petted.

Her eyes widened, and several incredibly long seconds later, she untangled herself from him as if he had fleas. Her body heat lingered even after she moved away.

Damon put his hands into his pockets to keep from touching her as much as to keep his cock in check.

"Listen, Tanika, that rodent's more afraid of you

than vice versa. Just stomp loudly and they won't hang around."

"Did you say *they*? And wait a minute . . . stomp?"

"Or dance. Or hop. Mix it up. It confuses them."

Her eyes narrowed and he fought not to laugh as he picked up the broom.

"This ought to keep you safe until I get back," he said, "but right now, I really need to get that generator started."

"Damon, why don't we just go back?"

To what? To the way things had been? Or did she mean back to the hotel? He chose the latter. "We can't go back because we're here and a few mice aren't going to scare us off. Right?"

She frowned. "They may have the freeway cleared by now."

"I seriously doubt it."

"There's got to be a way to get back to someplace civilized at the very least."

"Tanika—"

"Or we could stay at one of those cute little motels by the freeway exits—"

He gripped her shoulders and gave her a little shake, hoping to shed the rising panic in her voice. "Honey, the answer is no. I'm not going to risk getting stranded out there. We're here for the duration."

Her eyes were still filled with dread but there was stubbornness, too. "Fine."

"It *is* going to be fine . . . I'll go handle the generator and I'll be right back."

"Don't worry about me," she practically snapped. "I'll just . . . stomp!"

"Atta girl."

He turned and left before she had a chance to hurl something at his head. It wasn't until he was back with the generator that he started chuckling.

God, she'd made quite a sight balancing on that table.

And the way she filled his arms and dug her heels into his butt . . . that was just heaven. For once, he was glad for the cold.

It was odd, but he could've sworn that something had popped into her head at that moment. If so, what was that woman up to?

Tanika watched Damon from where she was cuddled up on the hard bench, wrapped in a thick blanket. Even with the blanket, she was so cold, her teeth were starting to sound like maracas. Twenty minutes had been enough time to inspect the room several times over, to dust off the furniture, and come up with her harebrained plan.

Not that it was much of a plan, but it was a surefire way to make her point. Without a doubt, this was the most harebrained thing she'd ever done in her life, and that included going to that Erotique Ball.

Since he'd entered the cabin, Damon had hardly done more than glance at her. Instead, he'd started a fire in the woodstove, and flipped a switch so that now a single soft-lit bulb outshone the candles in the room. More importantly, he'd found a small knot in the wood where the "rat" had disappeared and he was now hammering it closed. She might as well have been a piece of furniture for all the attention he was giving her.

"So, this is quite a place." She mentally rolled her eyes. Oh, yeah. Bring on the seductive talk.

He glanced at her over his shoulder. "Only when I need to get away from everyone and live the rustic life a little, which is very rare."

"How can you tolerate the rats?"

He shrugged "My manly screams scare them off."

"Ha, ha!"

He turned back, but she saw the smile on his face. "The caretaker usually cleans and vacuum-seals the place. They call him Zippy because he loves to seal-zip everything."

As evidenced by the blankets, towels, and even the mattress, the caretaker had to be obsessed with cleanliness—and the vacuum-packing machine—which at the moment, she really, really appreciated.

Damon continued to hammer in threes, driving the nails home. Wham, wham, wham. He used his flashlight to search around the room for any nail that was sticking out. As if he needed something, anything, to keep him from joining her on the bench.

His appearance was so different from the business-man she'd first met, that she simply stared at him. In his sweater, jeans, and rugged boots, he looked like a lumberjack. A sexy lumberjack. One who was set on nailing everything in the room but her.

"Does the generator mean we get hot water?"

"More like warm water. But give it an hour or so first."

"We have to share the same bed?"

"Unless you want to sleep on that hard bench."

She tucked the blanket to her chin. "You know what I mean."

All hammering stopped and he turned to her. "Whatever you're cooking up in that brain of yours . . . don't."

"Let's be realistic, Damon. We both know we can't exactly share that bed without getting intimate again."

He gave her an unreadable look, then went back to hammering. "Think again."

She was tempted to throw off the blanket then, but she held off. "You're kidding yourself if you think otherwise."

"Convenient for you, isn't it?" He grumbled to himself and finished hammering, then placed his tools on the table. "It's about seven-thirty. How about some soup for dinner?"

"No, thanks. I'm not hungry for soup." Tanika waited for him to ask what she was hungry for but he simply knelt by the woodstove to poke at it.

She tried to control her nerves, knowing it was

now or never. He'd just turned in her direction when she threw off the thick blanket with a flourish, revealing the scanty tiger-striped lingerie.

"Well, I'm all ready for bed. Wanna come?" She left the innuendo hanging. Her nipples were freezing and her teeth clenched tight against the cold. "I don't think you've delved into Nuclear Desire. It's the latest cream creation and it lives up to its name."

The last thing she expected him to do was to throw back his head and burst out laughing. He probably could not have laughed harder if she'd been wearing clown makeup and been blasted out of a cannon. He leaned against the wall, holding his belly as he roared.

It was amazing, really, how being utterly and completely pissed off could warm a body up, she thought.

"A simple 'no, thank you' would suffice!" she snapped, then snagged the fallen blanket, wrapped it around herself, and sat back on the bench, glowering at him.

That made him laugh harder, until she thought he'd break into tears. "God," he managed between laughs, "you're priceless."

"And you're a—a . . ." She clamped down on the jagged words that would only tick her off further.

He leaned his hands on his knees, like a weary marathoner, struggling to control his laughter until there were only a few occasional chuckles. "Sorry. Didn't mean to crack up—"

"Could've fooled me."

He rose to his full height, an unapologetic grin on his face. "You were standing there like some Nubian goddess, wearing that wild see-through number, and you were so cold, you were covered in goose bumps and your lips could hardly move."

Oh, that was just perfect! "Glad I could provide some entertainment."

A couple of deep-throated chuckles escaped him. "Now, Tanika, don't get all mad. It's just . . ."

"What?" So help her, if he laughed once more, she was going to grab the broomstick and whack away at his thick skull.

He tugged his ear, doing a bad job of forcing back his amusement. "It's not that I didn't expect a seduction scene, it's just that I hadn't expected such . . . dramatic flair."

"Forget it. I've changed my mind."

He moved in, or more like swaggered closer, all cockiness and good humor. "All right, let's start over. I'll pretend I didn't see that."

"Oh, go to hell."

He braced an arm on the back of the bench and another on the armrest next to her, effectively caging her in. His eyes gleamed with mischief and he nibbled his bottom lip, the urge to chuckle just barely under the surface, damn him. "You don't look so cold now."

She straightened as much as her seated position allowed. "I think I'll turn in for the night. Please move."

The humor began to seep from his expression.

"Tanika, I admire your healthy sexual appetite, but—"

"But what?"

"That doesn't mean I intend to be your human dildo."

"Excuse me?"

"Even your favorite dildo must have five memorable characteristics. Name five things about me . . . that have nothing to do with sex or work."

She blurted out the first things that came to mind. "Boats, and photography."

He shifted his stance. "And?"

"I'll bet you starch your underwear."

His lips twitched. "Is that the best you've got?"

"How about you? You think you can do better?"

"Absolutely. Starting with blueberry filling. You always grab the doughnuts in the meetings that have blueberry filling, which you somehow manage to eat without the slightest evidence of a mess. You like your coffee black and strong, with just a touch of sugar. You really like lingerie, which"—he raised a hand as she began to protest—"is an observation that has nothing to do with business. The fact that you had a career modeling intimate apparel is evidence enough. You indulge in cigars, drive fast, and just as intriguing, you can dance like a stripper. I really want to know more about that, but I think that's more than five things."

Tanika felt like she'd fallen backward on her ass. "You're observant."

"Did our terms and conditions for casual sex imply that I wasn't supposed to be observant?" Damon arched a brow for a full two seconds, which didn't settle her nerves one bit. "How's this for a new condition, Tanika? No sex."

She studied his serious expression. "I must've imagined that hard-on you had less than twenty minutes ago."

"No, you didn't. There's no doubt you turn me on. But until you remember five things about me other than the way we bump uglies, no sex. Surely we can live in this cabin for a night without it."

Tanika found herself blushing from the intensity and conviction in his eyes and the inexplicable embarrassment that swamped her. She looked away, only to notice the front of his jeans.

He stepped back, not bothering to hide his arousal. "Keep prancing around naked if you like. I don't mind."

"Maybe I will!" Turning on her bare feet, she made her grand exit by shaking her thong-wearing butt all the way to the bathroom where she closed the door with a firm thud.

The small room was even several degrees cooler. One look in the mirror and she knew why he'd laughed so hard. She looked like a mix between a stripper and a plucked chicken.

She leaned against the wall, gathering what was left of her brains and pride, and thought of an appropriate entrance. God, what was it about that man that caused her to behave so outrageously?

She was glad she'd thought to put her pink terry-cloth robe and bag of toiletries in the bathroom earlier.

Bundled up in her robe, she put the lid down on the toilet, then sat, thinking about her next move.

In a burst of motion, she turned on the faucets in the shower, shivering with relief when a few minutes later, the water turned warm.

She was shedding her clothes when the knock came on the bathroom door. "The water tank is small so don't use up all the hot water."

She stepped into the warmth, closed the shower curtain, and didn't bother replying.

The knock came again, louder this time.

"I'll be out in a minute."

It seemed like thirty seconds later, when the curtain was pulled back and Damon stepped into the tiny space, buck naked.

"What do you think you're doing?" she demanded.

"I don't like cold showers and I'd hate for you to hog all the hot water just to spite me."

"Why would I do that?"

"I don't know. You tell me."

He stepped under the stream of water.

"I think you've changed your mind."

"I didn't change my mind. Like I said, I want some of this hot water before you use it all up."

His fine, thick erection was practically knocking against her thigh. "That so?"

He had that stubborn but confident look on his face again. "Is that going to be a problem?"

"Not for me." She worked her scented soap over her breasts. Man, she ached for him. Having him this close and not touching him was pure torture.

"Mind getting my back for me?" she asked, handing him the soap.

He looked at the soap she dropped into his palm, then when he grunted a response, she turned her back to him, waiting. The first contact sent a tremor of heat down her spine, and she bit her lip to hold back the moan.

"Lean forward a bit."

She braced her hands on the tiles, all too aware of his hands washing her back and circling the flanks of her buttocks. They circled around the small of her back, in the same place he liked to hold her when she'd straddled his cock for an orgasmic ride. She waited for the contact of his lips on her back, but it never came.

When he finally said, "All done," his voice was gruff and husky.

"Thanks." She faced him, not taking the soap. "How about my front?"

"I think you can handle that yourself." He grabbed her hand and placed the soap in it.

"Want me to handle your front?" She rubbed the soap down his midriff, going for his rigid cock, but his hand stalled her.

"No, thanks."

"Then help me out. I'm a little cramped for space here." She moved under the water, slipped the soap back in his hand, then placed both over her breast, arching into him so that her hips grazed his cock.

A muscle twitched in his jaw, but he washed her breasts, then when she moved his hand down her belly and between her thighs, the soap slipped to the floor.

His breathing was already rough. "Oops."

"I could—"

His hand cupped her sex, stroking possessively over it, almost negligently, the look in his eyes cutting off her words. Instinctively, she widened her stance, shifting closer as his fingertips grazed her nether lips . . . once . . . twice . . . making them tingle even more as her pulse bloomed there. She wanted his finger to move deeper, but he wouldn't.

God, Damon . . . Oh, God . . . more! Just a little—

"All done," he murmured, removing his hand.

"Fuck!" Everything she craved poured into the word.

"I told you no." Holding her by her waist, Damon switched positions so he stood under the spray of water while she tried to recover.

As full-veined and plump as his cock was, he

made no move to resume the foreplay. Instead he briskly washed and rinsed in record time, then switched positions with her, putting her back under the tepid water before he stepped out.

"Thanks for sharing the hot water," he said.

She stood there, trembling with need in between flashes of cold air. She whipped the curtain closed on his smug face.

He chuckled, but he sounded pained. Good.

She heard the squeak of the door when he left, but she stayed under the shower until only the barest trace of warmth remained. A hand job wasn't going to do it. Not as aroused as she was. Her body ached for the weight of him, the masculine feel of his body hair, of his scent and taste against her skin. Of his fullness inside her.

Okay, so he had struck one underhanded, devastating blow to her plans. Or a couple. In fact, he'd deliberately turned her seduction completely upside down.

Crap.

Damon wiped the last of his ejaculation into his towel and leaned back on the bed, breathing heavily and seeing stars. Shit. He'd barely made it out of there in time.

He'd said no sex and meant it, but it had come damned close to the wire. It was all about the principle now.

He wondered how many unsatisfactory ejaculations were in store for him.

"Hell." He tossed the towel onto his laundry pile, tugged on some boxer shorts and a tank top, and began to drag the rickety metal bed closer to the fireplace, just close enough to still keep warm through the night. If the snow kept pounding them, the night would be a bone chiller.

Unless they snuggled.

Tanika stepped out of the bathroom, all soft and plush and perky in a silver slip that offered no protection against what was going to be a cold night. Her face was still that lovely flustered hue and her eyes were slightly glazed with incomplete desire. She did a quick scan of him and seemed to realize he'd taken matters into his own hands.

Hey, he'd given her time to do likewise. Why hadn't she taken care of herself in there?

"Look, I shouldn't have gone into the shower with you."

She waved away his remark and immediately grabbed a blanket, wrapping it around herself, obviously hell-bent on pretending nothing had happened. She cleared her throat. "What are you doing with the bed?"

"Moving it a little closer to the fire." He looked around. "Hungry? I have some snack food in the kitchen."

"Okay."

Moving in the awkward silence, he served up

some cheese, crackers, and canned fruit salad. Both grabbed a bottle of water, a fork, and began to eat.

Damon could see the signs of her sexual discomfort. She avoided his eyes, her lips looked swollen, and her racing pulse was clear at the base of her neck. She'd recrossed her legs twice and all but squirmed on the bench.

Still he couldn't bring himself to breach the tension between them. They cleaned up with little to say, and when she went to brush her teeth, he threw a few more logs into the woodstove and checked around the small room just to kill time.

He made sure she was settling into the queen-size bed when he went to brush his teeth.

With nothing more than a "good night," he turned the lights off and they lay in the bed, hugging the edges as if vipers lay between them.

Where were you last night? he wanted to ask. Did she expect him to accept that she could jump from his bed to someone else's, then back, without a problem?

As the sluggish minutes went by, the rusty light from the waning fire began to fade. He covered his eyes with one arm and punished himself with at least ten different ways of how his day could've ended.

Finally, exhausted, he relaxed into the mattress and allowed himself to sleep.

*T*anika heard the calm, even breathing and knew Damon was asleep. On the other hand, the state of her body's arousal had refused to abate and the need was steaming in her like a fever.

Between the cold silk of her slip and the diminishing warmth of the fire, her body was anything but relaxed. Reluctantly, she abandoned the bed to dig through her travel bag in search of more appropriate nightwear.

That was when she found the velvet handcuffs.

She twirled them on her finger, remembering she'd never gotten around to using them on him. The wild nights of sex she'd anticipated with him had always had a tenderness to them that had slipped into her soul.

This time around, sex could be just sex.

Grabbing them before she changed her mind, she walked back to the bed and noticed he had one hand next to his head and the other over his chest. He looked so damned masculine, and at the same time, so angelic . . .

She blew on her hands to warm them, then gingerly took the hand closest to his head and moved it toward the decorative iron reed of the old bedpost. With a quiet snick, the deed was done, and he was shackled to it.

Surprised that he was still asleep, she warmed her fingers again and moved his other arm a little bit at a time until he mumbled something and shifted his arm himself, closer, but not close enough.

She let a few tense seconds slide by before trying

again, and this time managed to handcuff that wrist to the headboard, too.

God, he was going to kill her.

The last part was the trickiest. She borrowed two curtain cords and, with freezing fingers, fashioned them into loops to be used loosely around his ankles. If he tried to kick his feet, the loops would tighten and secure him even further.

If only her Girl Scout troop leader could see her now, mastering the knots.

It proved to be very tricky to put the cords around his ankles but she finally managed it. Almost bubbling over with apprehension, she slipped off her thong and crawled back into bed, inching closer to him under the blankets until he stirred.

A frown came and went on his brow when she tentatively slipped her hand under his shirt, then down over the soft shape of his penis. His cock moved like a snake under her touch, swelling against her palm, awakening.

She stroked him carefully, growing just a little bolder when she felt him roll his hips, his erection hardening further.

Snuggling closer, she shifted a leg over his, hiking up her slip and riding the firm thigh muscle experimentally, still stroking him.

A clanging sound from the headboard revealed that he'd tried to move his hand. His frown reappeared, but a ghost of a groan escaped his lips when she stroked him again.

It was a delicate dance of caresses and careful motion before she had his cock partially out of the front seam of his boxer shorts.

She'd just shifted to straddle his hips when both handcuffs clanked louder as they hindered his movements.

His eyes opened groggily. "What the—"

She froze.

His eyes widened with incredulity.

"Shit." He bit the word off, jerking at his handcuffs.

"Now, Damon—"

"What are you doing?" he roared.

Reminding herself that she had a goal, she remained where she was, nothing but thin cotton separating his cock from her aching heat.

"I thought it was obvious," she replied, not sounding too certain of herself.

"Have you lost your mind?" His eyes were like daggers. "Don't you know what it means to take someone against their will?"

Heart thundering, she sat up more fully, letting the blankets fall behind her and then leaning forward so her cleavage was revealed. "Is it really against your will?"

"Why don't you take off these cuffs and I'll show you."

"The chemistry is there, Damon. Can you honestly say you don't want this?" She rocked infinitesimally against him, the very tip of his penis nestling against the damp folds of her sex.

"Damn you. You're so fucking desperate for sex that you're just going to take it? It's called rape, Tanika!"

She stilled above him.

"Goddamn you," he gritted through his teeth. "Undo these cuffs right now!"

"God, I'm sorry . . . I was just . . ."

He jerked hard against the cuffs, and she reacted by lunging for his wrists, ready to uncuff him before the feeble metal snapped.

In an instant, Damon turned his face into her breasts and sucked a nipple into his mouth, hard, taking it right through the satin and biting softly. A raw whip of desire lashed through her body, searing like liquid in her womb.

"Oh! Damon, please," she whispered, ashamed by the need in her voice.

She immediately rocked back, looking down at the stained wet spot where his mouth had been. Between her thighs, her clit bloomed and throbbed against the plump tip of his cock.

"Please?" she whispered, her mouth dry, her voice hoarse.

He studied her, his features a mixture of anger, desire, and caution. Either voluntarily or not, his erection pushed against her.

His eyes traveled like a caress over her face and

neck, pausing where the spaghetti straps held up the satin slip. "Lower the straps."

She did, slowly slipping her arms out and revealing her breasts.

"Put your breast in my mouth."

She lowered her left breast as instructed. Damon rocked and shifted beneath her, then wordlessly, she reached for his cock, inserting him into her clearly wet passage.

With little movement, they cleaved together, his thick cock filling and invading the slickness of her vagina, thrusting thickly inside her.

She held still, accepting the snug, solid flesh into her lubricated heat. His mouth sucked hard on her breast again, and she whimpered at the exquisite pleasure-pain. It pulled into her womb, into the other sensations that were curling and threatening to collide inside her.

He was angry still, but he wanted her. And he was letting her have him.

So, she tightened her legs around his hips and took him slowly, both liking and hating that she couldn't have more contact with his flesh than the front opening of his boxers.

He released the overkissed nipple and she instantly put her other nipple in his mouth; the jolt of that bite was almost too much to take. This time, when she pulled back, her nipple slipped from his mouth with an audible sound.

She pushed his shirt up, pushed the heels of her

hand on his chest, and ground out her need against his cock and hips. He thrust upward, responding with a predatory grunt.

The sexual dance began.

Every thrust he made swelled inside her, while outside, the cotton of his boxers rubbed against her sensitive clit, rough against her inner thighs. She felt overheated, surrendering inch by delicious inch to the surreal pleasure.

She rocked harder, forgetting where she was, forgetting the game, everything but the fact that Damon was beneath her, filling her and driving her insane.

The bed squeaked to the rhythm. Breaths echoed. Moans were muffled. Skin moved against skin, against cotton, muscles, and bone.

She heard a brief metallic screech and suddenly his hands were around her hips, holding her still while he half sat, pinning her against him, immobilizing them both.

"No!" She tried to move, desperate to cross that orgasmic divide. "Oh, God! Oh!"

Everything but her heartbeat seemed to have stopped and his lips brushed hers.

Instinct had her trying to complete their movements, but his strong arms held fast.

Half sobbing, she covered his mouth and he clutched her closer still, so hard and deep that it quaked in her gut and she gasped in midkiss, her orgasm imploding hard, almost violently, behind her eyes.

Her breath was his. Her body was his.

The moment was suspended endlessly. His, his, his . . .

Then in the juicy grip of her trembling vagina, she felt his hot ejaculation . . . taking her over with him again into a softer gentler undertow . . .

Time had elapsed again when she finally regained her senses and realized she was lying on him, her satin slip scrunched around her hips and his shirt pushed up to his armpits. The jingle of the broken handcuffs sounded like tiny bells when Damon drew the covers over them.

It had certainly not been the smoothest and most seductive thing she'd ever done.

But damn, it had been absolutely unforgettable.

Damon woke Tanika with a hard slap on her butt.

Startled and groggy, she practically sprang off his chest, then narrowed her eyes at him.

"Retribution," he said with a grin. "I plan on giving you half a dozen more."

She tried to scamper off but he rolled her beneath him, pinning her down with his weight. A gasp of shock escaped her when he pulled her hands above her head.

"Is this tit for tat?" she asked, sounding nervous.

Damon caught himself falling into the trap again, wanting to have her despite his original intentions.

"It's not about keeping score." He released her wrists but twined his fingers with hers. "I think you're scared."

She arched a brow, completely incredulous. "What?"

"You like sex, no doubt about that. But you're too scared to take more."

She tried to work her fingers free from his, but he held on. "I don't *need* more. Sex can be a meaning-ful relationship. Fulfilling, too."

"Sex is only part of it. What about the rest?"

She nipped his chin. "I find something I like, I stick to it."

He nipped her chin back. "You might be a sex addict."

"I would if you'd gimme some."

He studied her, holding her gaze. "What hap-pened to make you so gun-shy?"

She looked away for a split second, but he'd seen something in her eyes. "I don't know what you mean by gun-shy. I enjoy sex. It's physical. Your body, my body. We want the nookie. We crave the orgasm. It's a fairly enjoyable activity."

"The same can be said for dinner and a movie."

"Yeah, but then it gets messy."

"Messy?" He released her hands and stroked the soft skin of her cheek. "Did someone break your heart?"

Her pupils dilated with traces of guilt and embar-rassment. "Why would I let someone do that?"

"Why, indeed."

"If it's all about sex, there's no chance of that, right? Look, I'm a woman who basically knows what she wants, and right now, I don't want much more than a sexual relationship."

It wasn't entirely the truth. Damon could see her struggle in the depths of her defiant eyes.

"Whoever he was, he was a fucking idiot."

She glanced away, then back again. "Have you been listening to me at all?" she huffed, but he knew it was for show.

"Sex. Right. As you've proven, I like sex as much as you do. But you've got to tell me five things about me first, sweetheart. Until then, consider yourself on a sex diet."

He rolled off the bed in one motion, chucked off his soiled underwear, and found some fresh ones to wear.

When he turned around Tanika had the sheet to her chin again, a puzzled expression on her face. "Are you saying that if I come up with five things, we're back to sex?"

He found his T-shirt on the floor. "I don't mind helping you with your handcuff fantasy, or any fantasy for that matter, but as you pointed out early on in this relationship, I guess I really am a traditional kind of guy."

She still eyed him with confusion. "Why five things?"

"Why not?" The look on her face tugged at him.

Was she so determined not to let anyone close again that she thought she could treat him like her personal sex slave forever? "Why don't you think about it a while?"

He tugged on his thermals, jeans, and his thickest sweater, knowing he had to keep dressing or dive back into bed for what she offered. "We're running out of firewood. I think we have enough for one more night, but I need to check the supply."

She ran a hand over her hair and looked around.

"Um, want some breakfast first?" She sat up and her blanket shifted lower with the movement, enticing him with the unspoken invitation.

"Of course." He grinned. "I'd love some breakfast. With coffee, if you can find it."

She gave a brief smirk before scooting off the bed. "Do you know how many people would choose sex over coffee?" she grumbled.

Damon reached for his boots and began to put them on. "I have other plans than to end up as a frozen corpse with my hands tied to the headboard."

She shrugged, already banging pots in the kitchen, then glanced over her shoulder at him. "I promise to explain to the coroner about the smile on your face."

"Touché."

She looked over her bare shoulder at him, the blanket wrapped tight around her torso but dragging at her feet. The steel pot in her hand gave her an appealing air of domesticity. "About the, um, handcuffs? I'm sorry about that. I was selfish and—"

"It was unexpected."

She turned completely then, looking relieved and infinitely alluring. "I got a little caught up in it. Sorry if I, you know, stepped over the line."

He almost didn't know what to say to that, so he settled for, "I suffered greatly."

A lovely shade of red tinted her cheeks and at the last minute she looked away, whirling around to fill the pot with water. "As you should've."

Hope bloomed in his chest, and he found himself smiling as he did up the laces to his boots.

Tanika changed back into her slip and covered up with her robe. Damon downed the instant coffee she'd made with a weak cringe, then put on his ski jacket.

"Wait," Tanika called out when he was ready to walk out the door.

He paused with his hand on the knob.

"Here's one thing about you," she admonished. "You're missing a scarf or a hat." Having said that, she wrapped the terry-cloth belt of her robe around his neck, then raised her HIPHOP GIRL baseball cap to place on his head, but he stopped her.

"Got a watch cap," he said, placing the knit cap on his head. "Great scarf. Thanks." To her surprise, he pulled her in for a brief, sizzling kiss.

He left her dazed and licking her lips in amazement, the pink terry-cloth belt flapping in the curls of snow as he headed out for more firewood.

She stood there a few seconds longer, hugging the moment to herself.

Alone in the cabin, she cleaned herself up in the bathroom and changed into blue jeans and a red sweater. It only took a few minutes more to straighten the bedcovers and the room in general. When she was done she tested her phone, but the services were still down.

With little to do, she went into the kitchen, and debated over the cans of soup before selecting the minestrone for a light brunch.

She heard a few thuds from outside the cabin, and hoped it meant Damon was stacking wood next to the door. Then when some time went by without any stacking noises, she became worried. She threw the final three large pieces of firewood into the fire, then bundled up her jacket, intending to stick her head out the door, grab a bit more wood, and call Damon to lunch.

But when she opened the door, it was almost yanked out of her hand by the strong wind. A blast of snowflakes burst into the room, spraying into her face and pushing her a full step backward.

Before her, a wall of whiteness obliterated everything. The germ of worry spiked straight into full-blown fear.

"Damon!" Her shout was drowned out almost immediately. She stepped back in and forced the door closed, leaning on it, not daring to think of the possibility that Damon might be lost out there. Good God!

She jumped into action, throwing on her two sweaters and an extra pair of jeans. She remembered seeing a rope under the sink and went for it, pushing the thought of rats to the back of her mind.

This time she was a little more prepared when she ventured into the storm. Immediately, she tied one end of the rope to the post next to the door, calling out for Damon. Her fingers numbed so quickly, she could hardly secure the other end to her wrist.

With the rope in her hand, she moved out into the vortex of whiteness, the cold stinging her face. No matter how loud she yelled, it seemed that her voice didn't carry very far.

The snow now reached almost above her knees, and with each step that she took away from the cabin, the more she realized how unprepared she was.

She wandered back and forth, as far as the rope would allow, calling out for Damon. Only when the iciness became almost unbearable did she reluctantly start to head back on stiff legs.

She didn't feel the obstruction against her foot until it was too late, and then she was falling face-first in the snow. She struggled to stand, realizing for the first time that the rope had been yanked off in the fall and was no longer around her wrist.

chapter 14

Damon's bones felt completely frozen by the time he stepped back into the cabin and closed the door behind him. He looked around the small room for Tanika as he shook the slushy snow off his clothes. Even the socks he'd used for gloves were painful to remove from his hands.

Damned if that silly little scarf she'd given him hadn't helped, though. He made a beeline for the pantry, pulled out the bottle of whiskey that he knew was always there.

After fumbling to remove the cap, he took two large gulps of the fiery liquid, shuddering when the ball of heat landed squarely in his gut.

"Hey, Tanika," he called, expecting to hear her reply from the bathroom. When none came, he walked over and opened the door, finding no one there.

"Tanika?"

Nothing.

He searched the room, saw the bowls of soup on the table, and blinked in confusion. The second time he looked around, he noticed the cabinet door under the sink was ajar. He'd taken two steps in that direction when he suddenly remembered what he'd kept there and dread hit him like a ton of bricks.

"TANIKA!"

He ran for the door, pausing outside momentarily to check his neck chain for his mobile GPS unit. His heart jolted in his chest when he spotted the rope tied to the post, but when he pulled on it, only the wind's tug responded. Dear God, please, no . . .

"Tanika!"

He pushed through the snow, starting on a short grid around the house, hoping and praying she hadn't gone far.

Every second felt like an eternity. His voice was hoarse, his clothes were encrusted with ice, and his whole body was damn near shaking from the cold.

"Goddamn it, Tanika, where are you?"

He checked the GPS one more time and turned, moving into a perimeter check closer to the house. And that was when he found her, doubled over on the ground like a child, no more than five steps from the front door.

With renewed strength, he lifted her in his arms, carrying her back to the cabin, then kicking the door shut behind him. It flew back open like a child throwing a tantrum. Damon placed Tanika carefully in front of the fire and went back to shoulder the front door closed.

Knowing his own body was going to give in to

exhaustion soon, he worked as fast as possible. First he piled more wood into the stove, not caring if the place turned into a sauna. Right now, that was what they both needed. He'd burn the damned kitchen table later if he still needed firewood.

Next, he grabbed the whiskey bottle and, holding her head up, pressed the opening to her lips.

"D-d-drink up."

Her mouth parted, her teeth clattered against the glass, but he poured the liquid into her mouth, then cursed when she sputtered up most of it.

Drink it, honey. Come on. Again he poured the whiskey past her lips, and this time, even though she choked, she swallowed quite a bit of it, shaking slightly in revulsion as it went down. When she turned her head away, he took two large gulps for himself.

His muscles began to thaw, quivering with exhaustion and the ghosting sensation of heat, but he pushed the bed as close to the fire as safety allowed.

He stripped off his clothes, fighting the awkwardness of uncoordinated movements. He fumbled and cursed as he fought to undress Tanika, as well.

"D-D-Damon?"

Her whisper was so low and helpless, he fought the roil of fear in his gut.

"It's okay, babe," he managed through clattering teeth. *Stay with me, sweetheart. Please, stay with me . . .*

Two sweaters! Dear God, she'd doubled up on

clothes and gone out into the storm? Might as well
have tried to fly with a handful of feathers. What the
hell had she been thinking? He stripped them off,
clinging to his anger as he worked.

Once she was also naked, he pulled her up on the
bed, gathered all the blankets around them, and tried
to rub heat into her body, but the truth was, he wasn't
faring too much better. It was just so damned cold,
he felt as if he were nothing but hollow bones.

Muttering prayers in his mind, he held her close,
then realized they'd be warmer getting the direct
heat from the fire than insulating their coldness with
the blankets.

His brain felt like it was rapidly turning to sluggish mush, and his muscles were starting to spasm.
He couldn't lose her now, not when they were just
getting to know each other. Hell, she didn't even
know five decent things about him.

He groaned into the wet curls of her hair, her
breasts and arms molded to his chest, her hips and
thighs against his, all cold as cement slabs.

He lay there for what felt like an eternity before
the tingling in his fingers started to feel like fire.
Tanika, thank God, had stopped shaking so violently. The whiskey must've started taking effect because he felt lethargic and sleepy.

The hours melted away, sucking him into a state
of semidrowsiness. He vaguely remembered waking
up feverish, thirsty, and sweating like crazy. He felt
much more lucid when he dragged himself into the

bathroom to urinate, his muscles so weak he almost didn't make it. Then giving in to the intense thirst, he downed two bottles of water. It was harder to get Tanika to drink, but he was glad that she managed to finish a tall glass of water, fighting him all the while.

He lay back down, every joint and bone in his body aching. Darkness swirled in his head and he fought it until he had no choice.

When he woke up again, the room felt like a sauna, orange and black shadows reflecting on the walls and logs crackling in the woodstove. For a moment, he honestly thought he was in hell. He faded in and out of consciousness, waking to see different parts of the room in the same furnace light.

It seemed like much, much later that he dreamed of a cool, refreshing shower, and Tanika was wearing his Oxford shirt, beguiling him with her smile while her Naughty Devil tattoo winked at him.

"Okay, tell me about yourself," she murmured.

It was too surreal . . . all that perfection . . . all for him. "Fried bologna sandwiches. Love 'em," he heard himself saying, then wondered why he'd volunteered that particular piece of info.

Her laughter echoed in his head, and he reached for her, knowing only that he had to touch her.

Suddenly, the shirt was gone, and she was warm and sensuous against him, her body arched subtly. He was focused solely on her full breasts, luscious mouth, and womanly curves.

And he could drink from her, and drink and drink.

At first she tasted like cool water, and he could've sworn it dribbled onto his chest, but then she tasted like all woman, and he drank of her insatiably. He wanted his tongue on her sex, in her sex, between the feminine folds of labia, to that smooth, wet fruit of her vagina. He dreamed of the swelling bud of her clit on the roll of his tongue, of the tremble that came with the slow circular strokes he was sure would tear her apart.

He wanted it all, to be deep inside her wet heat, and yet to feel every tremor of her pleasure under his lips. His cock grew tight and hard, and he ground his hips against hers, pushing the tip against the folds of her sex. His testicles tightened and his hunger mounted.

Her soft moans merged with his deeper ones, her breath cooled him, burned him, and he simply took. It was more than the sheer mechanics of sex. There seemed to be no gravity, no fires, no hell, no cool showers of heaven. Just a surreal lightness, and the incredible slick grip of her sheath as he thrust into her . . . out, then in . . . again, fluidly, endlessly.

He filled his hands with her buttocks, buried his face in her neck, and reveled in the plump fullness of her breasts against his chest. Yes . . . yes . . . God, yes . . .

He moved slower, experimentally, so attuned to his cock that he felt each follicle of hair as it grazed her skin. He ground against her clit, taking her mouth as he would've possessed her lovely slit. His testicles gripped tighter. Her voice was louder now, higher in pitch, edgy with desperation. Her arms wound tighter around him, her thighs spread, then gripped tighter around his hips, resulting in the sweet, slick flex of her internal muscles, sucking the very length of his cock.

His lungs searing for breath, and despite the insane urge to postpone the inevitable, the blinding orgasm hit him like a supernova . . .

Even his toes curled.

He couldn't stop arching into her, drowning into the darkness of wet release that engulfed him, dragging him down, down, down . . . into the land of unconditional sleep.

Come on, you've got to have something to eat," his hoarse voice grumbled.

Something tapped Tanika's lips again and she turned her head slightly away, daring to open her eyes and look right up at Damon.

She'd never been happier to see anyone in her life.

"How are you feeling?" he asked.

She had to try twice before she could speak. "Like a noodle. A very weak, overprocessed noodle." Her voice was hoarse and it hurt to speak louder than a whisper.

"This will make you feel better."

His voice, she realized, was in the same shape as hers. She drank the spoonful of soup, groaning and flinching when the warm liquid went down, soothing her throat.

"I felt the same way," he said, scooping another spoonful for her, his hand not completely steady.

For a long while, she sat propped on the pillows while he fed her the minestrone. The woodstove was blazing again and there was a comfortable silence.

She was already feeling much better before she finished the soup. Damon set the empty bowl and spoon beside the bed and lay back down next to her, covering them with a blanket.

"Naptime again?" she asked, even though the very thought of it was already calling.

"We need to get most of our strength back before the road clears tomorrow."

"Tomorrow?"

"Mmm-hmm. Called to verify it."

She sighed. "Good." His face was taut, his cheeks bristly, and there were dark smudges under his eyes. But his eyes . . . they mesmerized her. With her head next to his, she could see every nuance of his pupils. His gaze held hers unblinking.

I thought I'd lost you! You scared the hell out of me! She wanted to say the words aloud, but instead, she touched his face, and when tears threatened, she settled next to him.

"You're not going to get all weepy on me, are you?" he asked, not bothering to hide a smile.

"It's not every day I get rescued from freezing to death."

"All in a day's work."

She blinked hard. "My hero. I'll try to control myself."

"Much appreciate it." He winked and shifted more comfortably onto his back.

"But seriously . . . Thanks."

He sighed. "Don't mention it."

"It's ironic, really. I went out there thinking you were lost."

"I knew where I was all along. I had the GPS unit I keep in my car. I mountain-climb and hike every now and then. It comes in handy. Keeps me from getting lost."

She sighed. Well, okay, that explained a lot. No wonder he hadn't needed her help. Hell, with that kind of endurance, he probably could've lasted out there longer than she could've.

"I know a couple more things about you now," she said, part of her hoping he'd fallen asleep.

"What's that?" came the tired rumble.

"You hike, mountain-climb, and like fried bologna sandwiches."

He tensed, then muttered an expletive.

She turned her head and met his wary gaze. "We . . . didn't have sex . . . did we?"

"We didn't?"

He momentarily closed his eyes and groaned.

"The best sex in the world and I'm the only one who remembers it?" she mumbled.

"I, ah . . ."

"Must've been delirious?"

"Exactly."

"Good. I thought I was the only one." She fell asleep with those words becoming hazy as they echoed in her head.

chapter 15

A shrilling ring had Damon sitting up from a deep sleep. The insistent sound grated on his nerves as it rang again, before he realized it was his mobile phone. He rolled out of bed naked and stumbled to the kitchen where he flipped the phone open. The bedsprings creaked as Tanika shifted.

"Hello?" he croaked, his throat as raw as if he'd swallowed steel wool.

"Damn, man, where've you been?"

"Dr. Wagner?" He recognized the voice and shook his head to clear it. At the same time, it dawned on him how very calm it was outside and he realized the storm had blown over.

There was a sigh on the other end. "Shit, I hate to break it to you like this, but your grandmother's in the hospital."

The world came to a halt and he felt as if he'd been poleaxed. "What?" he managed.

"Had some chest pains the night before last and the ambulance picked her up. She's at Mercy General."

Christ! Damon wasn't sure how long he stood there staring into space with the phone to his ear.

"You still there?"

He exhaled, and the world came back into cold, hard focus. "Yeah." His voice was no more than a gasp.

"Sorry, man. I tried to get a hold of you yesterday, but kept getting your voice mail."

"What floor is she on?"

"First floor. ICU."

Intensive care unit . . . "I'll be there in an hour."

"Damon—"

"Please tell her I'm on my way."

"I will."

Damon snapped the phone shut and noticed Tanika sitting up in bed. He jerked into action.

"Get dressed. I leave in five minutes."

She pushed her unruly curls from her face. "What happened?"

"Mrs. Becker's in the hospital," he said abruptly, then reached for his clothes. He couldn't say the word "grandmother" for the world.

He heard her sharp inhale but didn't respond to it. He couldn't, wouldn't, deal with anything more than getting to his grandmother's side and hoping he wasn't too late.

Thankfully, Tanika quickly left the bed, still looking a bit weak, but she dressed with urgency. He was done grooming in less than two minutes and began to carry his luggage through the knee-high snow to his vehicle.

By the time he got back, Tanika was dressed and ready, too. He hurriedly placed her luggage with his, and was infinitely thankful that she simply got in the vehicle without asking questions.

He started the car, warmed it up far less than the recommended time, and set it on four-wheel drive. It lived up to its reputation and plowed through the snow with ease. Half an hour later, he was cruising along the cleared freeway.

Out of necessity, Damon stopped at a gas station for gasoline, accepting the tall cup of coffee that Tanika placed in his hand without question. She'd also bought a couple of sports drinks and nutritious snacks.

"Thanks."

"Don't mention it."

He didn't speak again until they'd made it past the work crews that were busy clearing the road. And even then, it was only to mutter in frustration.

Unable to stand the silence for a second longer, she said, "Your grandmother is a tough woman. I'm sure she'll make it through."

The only change in his impassive expression was his brow furrowing a little deeper. "Let's hope you're right."

She kept quiet for the remainder of the trip back

to San Francisco, while he broke every speed limit in between.

When they finally parked in the hospital parking lot, he opened his door and paused abruptly. "Oh. Ah, I'll call a cab for you."

"Don't worry about me," she replied.

"No big deal. I can call—"

"I can take care of it."

"Thanks."

Distracted, he hurried into the hospital, with Tanika trailing not far behind. There was something about hospitals, she realized, something about the medicated air, the deserted hallways, and softly closing doors that made things seem precarious. In her experience, it was a church of a different kind, where prayers went hand in hand with pacing, and science often warred with time, hope, and faith.

Mrs. Becker was in the intensive care unit, where only family members were allowed, so Tanika waited in the lobby, watching the doors swing shut behind Damon's back.

Handfuls of people sat in the lobby, too, all with worried expressions, their thoughts seemingly in a holding pattern.

Tanika's stomach rumbled and she eyed a sandwich from a vending machine nearby, then decided against it.

Damon hadn't eaten since the oatmeal cookie she'd handed him with his coffee, so she knew he must be hungry, too. Tired and feeling invisible, she settled on the couch, waiting for him and praying for the elderly woman behind the doors.

Damon followed the nurse into his grandmother's room, unable to reconcile the image of his lively grandmother with the frail woman who lay looking so lifeless on the hospital bed.

IVs, monitoring devices, and oxygen tubes stuck out of her body like bizarre growths. She seemed to sink into the bed, and the more he looked at her, the more her wrinkles seemed to deepen, as if her body were aging right before his eyes.

He touched her hand, his own feeling numb. Her palm was paper dry, whereas his own were suddenly damp from nerves.

The nurse checked the drip, speaking softly when she explained that his grandmother was going to be resting for some time, but that he could stay.

After the nurse left, he pulled the spare chair next to the bed and held her hand. He should've expected this and stayed with her instead of taking off on a sex romp and leaving her all by herself. On New Year's Day, no less.

Shit.

If he hadn't been thinking with his cock, he would not have been so thickheaded about all her health issues, which were now so glaringly apparent.

The seconds were strung together by the beeps of a

machine nearby, grating with its low-level constancy. Her shallow breaths barely moved the sheets over her chest. She looked utterly fragile.

Happy New Year, Grandma.

In less time than he'd wanted, the nurse came in and asked him to leave, stating that "the patient" needed her rest.

He kissed her cheek and was led out into the cold, sterile lobby. He immediately spotted Tanika and his heart did a yearning kick that almost had his hands clenching into fists. She appeared tired and drawn but her eyes looked up at him, full of questions.

The anger that ripped through him was unexpected. If he hadn't been sidetracked by Tanika, he would've been at his grandmother's side. If he hadn't been tempted by lotions, garters, and lust he might've still been able to talk to his grandmother once more.

He was more than angry with himself and knew she was just the person to rip into for it.

Goddammit! He knew he was being irrational, but he couldn't stop himself from sitting away from her, not even glancing at her. "Go home."

Seconds crawled by before she replied quietly. "I want to be here in case you need me."

"I don't need you." His hoarse voice wielded the words like a sledgehammer.

Peripherally, he saw her hand flinch against the cushion, as if afraid she'd fall off the chair. "Then I'll just stick around to hear the word on your grandmother's condition."

He glared.

She glared back.

He shrugged. "Suit yourself."

He rubbed his eyes and settled in for the wait. Nurses came and went, always drawing his attention and stringing his nerves tauter. One family huddled by the door got good news, but the family sitting between him and Tanika were still waiting, their hands held tightly together.

He caught Tanika's gaze and absently wondered why she was still around. He turned away, waiting to hear the doors swing open again.

Hours must've passed but Tanika suddenly appeared beside him, handing him a soda and a large ham sandwich. Traces of her scent cleared the medicated air like a meadow breeze.

"Eat."

He eyed the heavy sandwich in his hand, not having the least appetite.

It didn't look deli fresh. It looked like it may have sat in a vending machine right up to its expiration date. Maybe even longer.

As if to prove to him that it was edible, Tanika opened her sandwich and began to nibble on it.

He sighed, tore off the plastic wrap, and bit into his sandwich. Not gourmet, but bland enough to chew on.

He swallowed and drank half his soda, feeling more human already. His sore throat had started to feel better, too. "Thanks."

They ate in silence for a while, then he stood and tossed the soda can and sandwich wrap into the garbage. He paused by the large window and looked over at the parking lot outside.

"You should go home and clean up," Tanika said, not far behind him. "I'll call you the minute something comes up."

"I'm not leaving."

"Then neither am I." She said it calmly, without rancor, then went back to the couch.

The hours started to crawl by again. The sun left its dialing shadow on the ground, covering tiles as the day grew. Damon practically twitched from too much coffee and not enough updates on his grandmother's condition.

Having Tanika in sight centered him somehow, and he felt a sudden shock when he was gazing out the window again and saw her reflection stand and move past the sliding glass doors . . . until she was out of sight.

He didn't think it was possible to feel emptier, but his body felt as if it were filled with lead as he made his way back to the couch.

It was his grandmother that mattered now. One thing at a time. He lowered his head into his hands and tried to push everything else aside and clear his thoughts. He simply couldn't handle much more.

About forty-five minutes later, he looked up when a large brown bag was dropped next to his shoes.

Tanika settled in the seat next to him, looking fresh and dressed in different clothes. Her hair was pulled back and she held something that smelled warm and delicious, which she handed to him.

"Eat."

"I'm not hungry."

"Eat it anyway."

He opened the bag and took a bite of the hot roasted chicken sandwich. Unlike the last sandwich, this one tasted like heaven and his appetite suddenly returned with a vengeance.

Tanika handed him a bottled water and nudged the bag with her foot.

"I got you some shaving supplies and a change of clothes. I had to guess at the size of the jeans, so I hope they fit."

Part of him rebelled, and he stopped gulping down half the bottle of water to ask, "Why are you doing this?"

She suddenly seemed intent on looking inside the bag as if to assure herself of its contents. "Just 'cause."

"Because what?"

She answered by placing a key into his hand. It was from a hotel right across the street from the hospital. Anger spiked so quickly he barely felt the teeth of the keys digging into his palm.

"What's this for?" he asked carefully.

Her eyes narrowed. "Certainly not for sex!" she hissed. "I'm doing all of this for your grandmother.

You look like you've just burst out of a mental ward and I thought it might be easier on her if you didn't walk in there looking scruffy and smelling ripe."

It shut him up, but he had to clench his teeth to keep from retorting.

Tanika raised a hand to silence him anyway. "Sorry. I'm out of line . . . But I just wanted to help."

She was right. He knew she was and it humbled him into uncurling his hand and accepting the key. "In that case, I appreciate it."

She nodded.

"Go on," she coaxed. "I'll call if anything comes up."

He left the lobby before he could talk himself out of it and hurried out of the hospital toward the hotel. He found the room easily enough and caught his gaunt reflection in the mirror.

It was all it took to start showering and shaving.

He nicked his chin in two places, but he was a sight better without his five o'clock shadow. The shower had revitalized him significantly, especially since Tanika'd thrown toothpaste, a toothbrush, and deodorant into the bag.

The blue jeans fit about right, but the blue flannel shirt was snug around the shoulders and biceps. It was clean and it fit, and at the moment, that was all that mattered.

He returned to the hospital, needing to see not only his grandmother, but Tanika as well.

chapter 16

*T*hat evening Tanika was glad to see the nurse walk into the room and call Damon to inform him that his grandmother was awake.

Damon had been talking to Cindy's husband, and Tanika had been in the process of helping her sister fix the hole in the blanket she'd been knitting. At the news, even Bubba had glanced toward the nurse.

When Damon and the nurse left, Cindy shifted her son in her arms, and raised both eyebrows at Tanika. Her husband knew better than to interrupt.

"So, how long have you two been doing it?"

"Excuse me?"

"Oh, come off it. Every two seconds, you're looking at him like a lovesick calf."

"Geez, Cindy. A cow?" Tanika worked the knitting needles, easily fixing the last hole in the blanket and keeping her eyes on each stitch even though she could've finished the blanket with a blindfold on.

"I promised not to give you the Big Girl lecture, but Tanika, really. What the hell were you thinking, sleeping with a business partner?"

"God knows I don't need to hear this right now," Tanika sighed.

"Well . . . My goodness." Cindy's voice softened. "You really fell for him . . ."

Tanika looked up, about to deny it, and wondering what her sister had seen in her to make the comment.

The need to reveal her lonely secret burned in her chest. "Fell? Hardly."

Cindy exhaled, fluttering her own bangs.

"Well, okay. More like a full-on, double back-flip dive from a very tall cliff."

"Oh, Nika."

The sympathetic tone almost made Tanika bare her soul. "Girl, it's not tragic. I mean, I'll get over it, right?"

Cindy shook her head and hugged her. "You haven't told him?"

"No. We agreed not to mix business with pleasure."

Cindy did a double take. "Okay." But she might as well have added the words, "That was stupid."

Tanika exhaled, folding the knitting away. "Please, no lecture."

"Wouldn't dream of it. I'll just pray that your double-flip dive has a soft landing."

Damon thought he was prepared for the frail woman on the bed, but this time she was awake, and her weakness only made her seem more helpless.

He'd been warned by the nurse to make it brief, so he greeted his grandmother with his widest grin and sat on the side of the bed.

"Hey, Nana." He touched her arm where it lay like a twig on the bed.

"Hey yourself," she replied, her voice practically a whisper.

He touched her hands, giving them an awkward pat. "That must've been some dancing you did on New Year's Eve to end up here."

She closed her eyes but smiled. "You bet. Drank just a touch of champagne and listened to Thelonious Monk."

Ah, yes. Thelonious Monk had been her husband's favorite musician. When he was a child, it had been a big deal for Damon to be allowed to touch his grandfather's vinyl records.

"What about you?" she asked, peering at him again.

Had lots of sex, wore stupid wings to a costume ball, and ended up snowed in at a cabin.

"We watched the fireworks and drank champagne."

She licked her dry lips. "We?"

"Want a sip of water?" he asked, already reaching for the cup with a straw on the bedside table.

"Mm-hmm."

He raised it to her lips and she took birdlike sips. But after he placed the cup back, she repeated her question.

"Yes, my date," he replied, unsure if telling her the truth would only aggravate her.

Her eyes softened. "You mean that woman that left you smelling like white ginger?"

He resigned himself to a nod.

"You mean Tanika."

Oh, she knew! "That would be her."

"I see." Nana sighed and closed her eyes momentarily, still smiling wistfully. "She must be special for you to take her up to Tahoe with you."

Despite his rioting emotions, he had no doubt about that. "She is."

"Good. I've always wanted you to find someone special. Someone to love."

Love? "I didn't say that."

"You didn't have to." She briefly squeezed his fingers. "You've got that stupefied look on your face."

She started to laugh, then winced in pain. Damon popped out of his seat, hovering and not knowing quite what to do.

"Sit, sit . . ." she finally gasped. "I just forget I'm old. At least my heart is."

Damon tentatively sat, hoping that the unchanging chirps of the machines meant that things were more or less normal and under control.

"I should've been here with you," he said, his heart heavy.

"Nonsense. You followed your heart and I'm proud of you. Wanted you to know that."

Jesus Christ, her words sounded so final! It tightened his already hoarse throat. "Get better so you can tell me all about it at our next Monday morning meeting."

Her eyes drifted shut. "Might have a change of plan. Jamus is waitin' . . . and I've missed him so much. Very much."

He swallowed hard, hoping it was the medication that was talking. "I love you, Nana."

Her eyes opened a crack. "Love you, too."

He rubbed her hand until her eyes drifted shut again and the nurse came to the room.

"She'll likely sleep for most of the night, but you can visit again tomorrow," the nurse informed him.

He found himself back in the lobby, like a prisoner led back to the jail cell. Tanika was instantly at his side.

"How is she?"

"Tired. Drugged." He shook his head, unable to explain the sense of doom that had remained with him.

He sat down on the couch again, exhaling a puff of air, then rubbed his eyes.

Cindy and her husband graciously offered their help, but then said their goodbyes when their baby wouldn't stop crying. Other friends of his and his grandmother's came by to give him support. Throughout the whole time, he was aware of Tanika at the edge of it all, looking more exhausted than he'd ever seen her. Nonetheless, she sat in the far couch, knitting the baby blanket her sister had started.

The gentle click of the needles skipped a beat when she met his gaze, but she resumed knitting. It seemed like a relaxing thing to do, but then again, Naughty Devil made about ten different muscle-relaxing, stress-relieving lotions. Chances were she even had half a dozen of them in her purse.

"Go home," he said.

"No."

He shrugged and tuned her out, focusing on the ICU doors again, waiting for the moment when they would open for him.

Tanika groggily woke up when her pillow shifted, except it took a few more seconds to realize it wasn't a pillow at all but Damon's arm as he'd stood. When had he come to sit beside her?

A male doctor was talking to him, and Tanika blinked to attention, standing on tired legs. Somehow, the blanket she'd finished knitting had been covering her, but she barely noticed it fall to the ground when the doctor said, "I'm sorry, Mr. Becker."

"Sorry?" Tanika echoed in a whisper.

"She went peacefully," the doctor said, perhaps repeating what he'd said to Damon.

No, no, no . . .

She watched Damon sit down as if in slow motion. She touched his shoulder, but he immediately shrugged it off, like a pesky fly. Hurt, she stepped back, watching him turn into himself, closing the world off, until he seemed perfectly isolated.

She sat a short distance away, having retrieved the small blanket and holding it in her lap and wanting more than ever to ease his pain.

"Damon?"

He turned at the sound of her voice, dismissed her with a vacant look in his eyes.

"I have to go," was all he said before walking out the door.

chapter 17

Tanika went back to the hotel room, unsuccessfully fighting tears and sorrow as she made some calls to inform her sister and some of their close associates of Ms. Becker's death.

That done, she kicked off her shoes, curled up in the bed, and mourned the passing of a woman she'd admired. Right then, Tanika decided she'd name a line of lingerie in her honor. Damon might not like the idea but that wouldn't stop her. It was not something she was going to change her mind about.

The tears moistened her cheeks, then eventually dried tight on her cheeks. She fell asleep again, wondering about Damon, worrying, wishing things had turned out differently.

Deep in the night, she was roused when the door opened and Damon's familiar shadow moved through the doorway. The door closed again and there was nothing but darkness again.

She reached over and turned on the bedside lamp, cautiously moving off the bed and toward him. He looked like a man holding back demons, as if he'd tried to exorcise them and failed.

"I knew you'd be here." It sounded like an accusation.

When she didn't reply, he asked, "Why are you here?"

"You must've known I'd come."

He tossed the keys on the dresser and tugged his shirt from his jeans. "Of course."

"Damon—"

"Don't talk. I'm all talked out anyway. We're good when we don't talk."

He practically ripped his shirt off, his eyes hard with intent. Tanika hadn't realized she'd crossed her arms protectively over her breasts until he sneered.

"Why else would you be here, Tanika? You could've gone home by now, could've been sleeping in your own bed."

"So could you!"

"And yet here we are. Must be for the sex."

He prowled closer, shucking his jeans and underwear in jerky, angry movements, his muscles tensed, his erection swollen and toned.

"No." The word stuck to her throat.

"Don't talk, goddammit. Don't say a fucking word."

He pushed her against the wall, gripped her hair in one hand and covered her mouth in a punishing kiss. There was nothing gentle about it, just savage need. His breathing was harsh and jagged against her face, his mouth tasting of unseen tears.

Tanika went limp beneath him, hardly able to respond and determined not to fight him or incite him further. As if bent on destruction, he yanked at her shirt, tearing it in his haste to remove it. She helped him take off her jeans only when the garment began to cut into her hips.

His strong fingers gripped, molded, searched her skin as if he could reach beneath it to her bones.

Abruptly, he maneuvered her onto the bed, covering her before she could move. He positioned himself between her thighs, starting to push the rigid length of his cock against her sex, into it. Tanika shoved hard against his chest.

"Damon, no! If you need me to help you let go, just tell me. But don't do this, babe."

"I don't need you!"

It cut. God, it cut. "I know."

His eyes locked with hers then . . . dark pools of sorrow and regret that shimmered with tears, his soul beckoning to her. He closed his eyes and held her immobile, his whole body stiffening.

Even as she watched, a tear slid down his cheek and he shifted his hips away from her, turning her into his embrace and holding her so tightly she could barely slip her arms around him. Everything about him smothered her . . . his body, the intensity of his sadness, and the losing struggle for control.

His ragged sobs were muffled against her hair, his arms all but breaking her ribs.

Tanika also mourned, cupping his head, kissing his neck, and trying to comfort him with words that felt incredibly inadequate.

It seemed like hours that they lay there together, naked in the cold room, the silence broken only by tears and memories. At some point, her tattered voice had given up and her words had become raspy cooing sounds that faded away in the room. Damon's arms eased their viselike grip, but remained around her, shifting every now and then for a brief caress.

When she shivered, he reversed their positions and covered them with a blanket. Tanika lay there awake for most of the night, aware of her legs straddling his thigh, and his limp penis by her hip. His strong shoulders were reflected in the white porcelain of the bedside lamp, which also reflected her expression, but not his face.

She listened to the rhythm of his heart beating beneath her ear, knew he was also awake.

His hand came around to hers, covering it where it lay against his chest.

"Want to talk?" she asked into the silence.

He exhaled, the breath pulling from deep in his chest. "I'm sorry."

"No apologies necessary." She tipped her head up to his weary, handsome profile. The ghosts of sadness were still in his eyes. "Tell me about your grandmother."

"I'll get to that." His free hand cupped her head gently this time. "But I wanted to say I'm really sorry for the way I came at you."

A mixture of emotions swamped her. "Forgiven and forgotten."

"No. I've never done anything like that in my life. I deserve to have my ass kicked. I just wanted . . ." He exhaled and she knew what he meant. He'd wanted the mental and physical release of sex, the escape of falling apart without the sorrow.

"I had no right to say the things I said, much less do the things I did. I was angry."

"At me," she guessed.

"Mostly at myself. I knew my grandmother's health was getting worse." His fingers moved to the back of her neck, massaging.

"But you blame yourself for taking off to Tahoe with me instead of staying here with her?"

Even now, she could see he had trouble answering. "Yes. She never let me down. She was there whenever I needed her. Always. And this time, I let myself get caught up in sex instead of being there for her."

Caught up in sex . . . not caught up in you.

"You were there for her, Damon, whether you'll admit it to yourself or not," she murmured firmly.

"Thanks." But a frown returned to his brow and he looked away, falling back into his thoughts.

Tanika laid her head back on his chest and Damon absently resumed massaging the back of her neck.

No matter what happened between them now, she was glad that he'd come to her after all. That she'd been able to comfort him, if only for a while.

A few hours later, they moved together under the sheets, Tanika dreaming of love and Damon craving the heat and taste of her. He willed himself not to care too much, but in the total darkness he forgot about grief and death, and under the spell of her touch, Damon felt the world heal and his soul settle where it belonged.

It was like they'd never been lovers before. Every caress seemed undiscovered, their movements faltered a little, becoming new and much more uncoordinated compared to the previous encounters.

He came with his pulse drumming in his veins and her breath shaking on his ear. "I love you . . ."

He could've sworn she'd said the words, but as he caught his breath, he was equally worried he had imagined it. It snagged like a fishhook into the moment.

"What did you say?" he asked when he could breathe.

He counted seven heartbeats before she wearily replied, "Nothing."

Nothing?

All the events of the last few days clustered together in his mind and he knew he had to draw the line. He couldn't go on this way, couldn't want her, crave her, and want a life with her when that was not where she said the relationship was headed.

No. He had to step back and reevaluate things.

Right now, he was flying blind, his instincts muddled, his emotions more than likely something that she didn't share.

If he declared his love now, would she think he was reacting to his grandmother's death? Or would the words "no strings attached" pop into the conversation?

Maybe he would've done things differently, changed the rules initially. Or maybe he could've told her how he felt in the cabin before the news of his grandmother had struck. He wanted to believe that she'd stood by him because she was more than a friend. But was it love or was grief clouding his judgment?

Unable to sleep, he stepped away from the bed and washed up, dressed, and brewed a pot of coffee that tasted expired.

By the time she sat up in bed, he'd been sitting on the chair by the bed for hours, having contemplated the next step and resolving to see it through.

He watched Tanika wake in degrees, then reach over the sheets to him, only to stop and pop her head up groggily.

"Crap." It was said in such a heartfelt way that Damon found himself grinning.

She buried her face in the pillow, then flopped onto her back, before sensing his presence.

"I thought you were gone," she said into the stillness.

"I didn't want to leave without saying goodbye."

"Oh." She tugged the sheet up to her chest and sat up some more, waiting a moment before asking. "That smells so good. May I have a sip of that?"

He walked up to the bed and handed his mug over. "It's not the best in the world."

She drank it like it was, taking two large gulps before handing it back.

"I have a bunch of things I need to get started on . . . mostly the funeral plans," he explained.

"I can help."

"No, thanks. It's something I need to do myself."

They sat in awkward silence for a few more minutes.

He cleared his throat. "Thanks for last night."

She looked like she didn't know what to say to that, other than responding with a faint shrug of her shoulder and a quick weak smile.

He placed the empty mug by the dresser. "Tanika, I don't see how we could work out."

She swallowed. "I didn't ask for promises."

"I know." Except he still wasn't sure he understood why.

"You're a wonderful woman with so much to offer."

Her eyes became deadpan. "Offer to someone else?"

"No, that's not what I mean. It's what gets offered that ultimately matters."

Her eyebrows went up. "Let me guess, you want to be friends and all that."

"No. And stop putting words into my mouth."

Her weak smile almost made him return to the bed. "Please don't do the it's-not-you-it's-me routine. If you have to go, just go."

He looked into her eyes. "I need to know where we are headed, if there's a future for us. And all I can say is—"

"Don't."

"Don't what?"

"Let's make it a clean break."

He felt like he was turning into stone again. "Why?"

Her voice was raspy when she spoke. "Because you are still grieving and you're going through a huge emotional upset. I wouldn't want you to say anything that you'll regret a few days from now. It's been a lovely and hectic week, really, and I'd rather have you walk out that door than say something you really don't mean."

"I'm a grown man, Tanika. I think I know my own mind."

"Earlier, you were so caught up in grief, even you admitted you weren't thinking straight," she pointed out.

He took a deep breath and closed his eyes. Did she think he couldn't tell grief apart from love? Or did she just not want to hear him complicate things by declaring his love?

I love you! He almost spoke the words.

"Just say goodbye, Damon."

He walked numbly to the door, pausing with his hand on the doorknob. "Goodbye."

"Bye."

He closed the door silently behind him.

Nika! The baby bottle goes in Bubba's mouth, not his eye!"

"Oops, sorry!"

Cindy huffed over and all but snatched her son from Tanika's arms. "There, there, honey. Your auntie's got her head in la-la land again."

"I told you I don't do babies," Tanika grumbled, knowing she was at fault.

"It's easy. If you'd looked down, you'd see that the baby bottle goes in his mouth. How hard can that be?"

"Sorry."

"Are you gonna snap out of it or do I need to do an intervention?"

"What are you talking about?"

"Don't give me that! You forgot to pick up your stuff from the cleaners and they ended up calling me about it."

"It's not a crime to have a faulty memory."

"You never forget anything that has to do with clothes. And you're moping."

"I don't mope."

"Your face is draggin', your ass is saggin'."

"Now you're just being mean."

"Damn straight. You practically begged me to start work two days ahead of schedule, which just so happened to coincide with the day Damon started back to work."

Tanika stood and reorganized the fruit in the fruit basket. "You know, just because you qualify to be a nagging wife, doesn't mean you get to be a nagging sister, as well."

"Now look who's being mean?"

Tanika made a face at her sister, then decided the bananas needed to be at the bottom of the fruit pile after all.

Cindy noted the restacking by pursing her lips, but she pressed on. "So, what's the deal? What's going on between you two?"

"Nothing."

Cindy dabbed the napkin at the milk spilling on her baby's chin. "Want to know how Damon is doing?"

Yes! Even the sound of his name made her heart lurch in her chest. "Cindy, really . . . only if you feel the need to."

"I don't."

Damn.

"But you two are like the face-saggin'-butt-draggin' twins."

Tanika pushed her braided hair from her face. She'd recently had her hair braided again, and the tight pain of it matched the tightness in her chest. "Cindy, why am I here? No matter how much I try, I can't babysit worth a damn and I don't have anything to do with Becker Fine Tailoring anymore."

"He's asked for you."

"Damon? Why?" God, did her voice really squeak like that?

Cindy grinned, her eyebrows raised. "Business. He was under the impression you were going to help on the Valentine's Day launching."

Tanika gripped the counter and counted to seven before snapping, *"And?"*

Cindy made a face. "Thinking swiftly, I told him no. I mean, you obviously didn't want to hang around and—"

Tanika gasped. "You said no? How come you've never mentioned this before?"

"I'm bringing it up now, aren't I?"

Tanika casually plunked down next to her sister. "Well, what did he say?"

Cindy's expression became even more smug. "That you had some great ideas and he was wondering if there was more where they came from."

"Of course I have great ideas."

"Well, I chose to assume he was talking about work rather than y'all's sex life."

Tanika rolled her eyes. "How does your husband put up with you?"

"The same way you do. I'm lovable."

"Marginally." Tanika straightened the blanket next to her. The one she'd knitted. The one Damon had once covered her with. Displeased with her train of thought, she folded it.

"Okay, here's the thing, Tanika. I was actually half lying. I told him I could probably get you to put in some final touches."

One look and Tanika knew Cindy wasn't joking. "Without asking me?"

"We all know you're the perfect person for this. And besides, if you're over him—like you claim you are—this should be no problem."

Bubba belched as if to emphasize the remark.

Cindy automatically blotted the baby's lips. "So are you in or out?"

She tried to stare her sister down while arguing with herself that it was *crazy* to even contemplate going back to Becker Fine Tailoring. Damon would be there every day! She had to be out of her mind! Nuts!

"Fine." She marched to where her purse sat. "I'll see you Monday, but you'd better not try to play any of these games at work."

Cindy gave her a happy little wave. "You're welcome, sweetie."

Tanika gave her a final glare, then left. She sagged against the closed door for a second longer, suddenly feeling nauseated and a little frightened.

* * *

Since the moment she'd shown up at work, Tanika kept it professional. She'd worn her most reserved suit, and from head to toe she'd made sure every accessory was sharp, neutral, businesslike.

Sure, her knees had threatened to buckle when she'd seen Damon. He looked a little gaunt since the last time, but his whiskey-brown eyes were still pools of emotion. Part of her wanted to rush up to him and hold him. The other part had her leaning against a nearby chair, praying she could hold herself together long enough to keep from humiliating herself.

It helped that he was equally formal, professional, and as courteous as a butler. But those eyes . . .

No, sir, she wasn't going to try anything stupid again.

She could get over him.

She would.

Even if it meant flirting with every other man in the room.

Damon had made it easy by giving her instructions about what he expected—"elegant, a touch traditional, and sensual sophistication"—then left.

He'd given her a stack of photographs to work from, or as he'd said, "for inspiration." Right off, she decided to frame the ones of his grandmother as a young woman, holding on to a man who was quite possibly Damon's grandfather. Both were laughing while he spun her around in his arms. There were a number of them, slightly more recent, of his grandmother with her arms wide open, as if she could embrace the fireworks that were blazing in the sky above her. Then there was the last photo, a close-up of her own thigh, where her tattoo had been colored over until it looked neon red.

Damon, Damon . . . what are you doing to me?

Tanika stared at the photo for a long time, realizing then that she had to incorporate a little of everything into the window display, even if there were some selfish reasons involved.

chapter 18

*T*anika's heart thundered as she reviewed her work in the private room she'd been given to work in. Well, "private room" was a bit of a stretch. It was more like a spare room that warehoused excess display items.

Squinting her eyes, she tipped her head and tried to view it through Damon's eyes. It had taken her almost two weeks, and three of his top specialists, to get all the elements right. But suddenly, she had a case of nervous uncertainty.

The display booth had been bathed in yellow, red, and silvery blue silks. A female mannequin had a devilish gleam in her eyes and a wicked, joyful grin. She was holding her hands out to where tiny lights imitated heart-shaped fireworks. The ND earrings were a striking touch, matching the black nylons with the tiny trademark icon at each of her ankles.

Behind her was the cool male mannequin, pristine in his executive-cut suit. She'd kept him hairless and stern. Truth be told, she'd thought about adding angel wings to him for kicks. Just for a second.

Thank God the temporary madness had faded.

He stood with the female mannequin's navy blue blazer in his hands, in such a way that he could either be flinging the jacket open at any minute or holding it firmly closed. The mechanism on his arms made the material shift just enough to cause the viewer to wonder uncertainly.

This was the delving tease.

Every fifteen minutes or so, the male mannequin's arms opened the jacket wide, revealing some of their hottest-selling lingerie. Other times, it would close the jacket tight, and the lights would temporarily dim, causing the fireworks behind the inanimate couple to glow brighter.

There were bursts of women's underwear around the room, twirled into bouquets of flowers and popping from rockets. Words like "delve," "crash," "hot," and "naughty" were strategically placed.

Feather ticklers added an exotic touch, and the result was a portrait of a woman who looked like she was rejoicing in sensuality, and yet was cherished by the man behind her.

But would Damon see it that way?

Would he understand what she was trying so desperately to say?

Sighing, she sat on the fancy French lounger behind her and eyed the lights. Maybe she should've gone with fewer lights. But who enjoyed mediocre fireworks? No, the lights stayed.

"Geez." She rubbed her forehead. There was no

room for improvement now. It was what it was. He'd either love it or hate it.

But she was pretty sure his grandmother would've loved it, and that had been the whole idea. Tanika smiled.

She relaxed into the lumpy furniture just as she heard the door open.

She was expecting it to be her assistant perhaps, but when Damon walked in, she sat up, waiting with bated breath.

Damon felt like he'd stumbled into a dream. His attention was riveted on the colorful display, remembering the bulky camera in his hand only when it started to slip out of his grasp.

It got so quiet he could hear the hum of electricity when the display converted yet again into a fireworks show. The male mannequin's arms embraced the female, trapping her, seemingly enthralled by her.

There was a tiny movement to his right and he turned, noticing Tanika for the first time. The fake fireworks painted her face in soft light, revealing her apprehension.

"It's perfect."

She released the breath she'd been holding, smoothing her skirt before replying. "Thanks. Your assistants had a lot to do with it."

Bull. There were too many personal touches that could've only come from her.

"Mind if I take pictures?"

"Not at all."

Raising his camera, he began to take pictures of the display.

Several shots into it, the male mannequin pulled the jacket wide open, revealing the negligee for about a minute before covering up again.

Damon chuckled and continued with the photos. Finally, satisfied that he'd captured the multiple facets Tanika had intended, he shifted the camera, turning it toward her.

"Stop!" She put her hand out as if he'd whipped out a gun.

He paused. "I once told you there was a next-to-last thing I wanted to ask you, but I never got around to it."

Not giving her a chance to reply, he pressed the button, the sound louder than her gasp.

"Mr. Becker, if you think—"

"I want to ask it now." He lowered the camera just enough to look directly at her.

She nervously licked her lips. "This isn't work-related."

"You're right. It's not."

She reached blindly for her purse. "Well, that's the only relationship we have."

He turned his camera off. "Why? Because you said so?"

Her back stiffened. "We said our goodbyes, Damon."

He shook his head and moved closer to her.

She turned in exasperation, going to the nearby controls and turning off the display. With two flicks of her fingers, the room was flooded with harsh fluorescent light and the fake fireworks faded.

Damon moved toward her again. "I knew you were pushing me away but I didn't know how to stop you. You stood by me all the way to the end. Why did you close me out?"

Her chin quivered ever so slightly. "I'm a woman of my word. I said I'd go into it with no strings attached and that's how I ended it."

God, she was something. Something wonderful. He touched her chin and when she didn't shy away, he kept his hand there. "I've kept your picture in my wallet. The one where you look like you're thinking of us together. So I want to know the truth. Why are you here?"

Several seconds went by. "Damon, I'm only here because of what your grandmother meant to me."

"Come on, now. Is that the whole truth? I'm only here because I'm crazy about you."

She tucked her chin down, away from his touch. "Stop it. Just stop."

"Darling, this is one of those times where stopping just might kill me."

She peered up and he could see the tears building in her eyes.

"Why did you go after me in the storm, Tanika? You risked your life that night. Why?"

She clenched her jaw, her voice even. "It's what any decent human being would do for someone."

He leaned so close to her that his nose almost touched hers. "You told me you loved me."

The light was perfect for revealing her panic. "No, I didn't."

"You did."

"Absolutely not!"

"Am I so unlovable?"

"Jesus!"

It was killing him to resist her lips. "Well, to me, you're pretty lovable. In fact, I've come to realize that there's no cure for having fallen crazy, deeply, and totally in love with you. You don't want to hear me say it, but there you have it. I love you."

She closed her eyes for a full second, her breath exhaling softly. When she opened her eyes, her lips formed a weak smile and a tear slid down her cheek. "I'm completely wrong for you."

"You're perfect for us. In fact, I want to get to know every part of you until we're both old enough to argue about the good old days."

He kissed her again, just a touch on her lips to give him the strength to say, "It's not about sex clubs, New Year's or Christmas or any of those things, love. It's about forever with you."

"Oh . . . Damon . . ." She smiled tremulously.

"Go ahead. I dare you to break my heart."

"You know I can't!" She wiped at her happy tears. "I love you so very much."

He picked her up and whirled her around, cutting loose with a loud army hoot before saying, "Marry me."

Her eyes widened even more and her face beamed. The diamond ring in his palm glistened and winked in the light.

"Oh, my God . . ."

"Make me the happiest man in the world and marry me, Tanika."

She nodded, her hand over her mouth in surprise as he slid the ring on.

"I'm going to assume that's a yes?"

"YES! Yes! Yes! . . ." She jumped up at him and he kissed her soundly, sealing each word with love and laughter.

"Promise?"

"Yes!"

"Forever?"

"Yes!"

He spun her around and cheered at the top of his lungs.